Midnight was hurt—she had to help him!

There was a sickening, splintering crunch, and Ashleigh whipped her head around to see Midnight toppling over backward. Sparky backed away as the black horse flailed on his back for a moment, whinnying hysterically. Ashleigh couldn't believe her ears. The screeching, high-pitched whinny that rose and filled the air was like nothing she'd ever heard before. Finally Midnight scrambled to his feet, reeling sideways and teetering painfully on three legs. His right hind leg was hovering above the ground.

Ashleigh felt sick to the bottom of her stomach, frozen to the spot. *It's Midnight's leg—he's hurt it badly*, she thought, hoping it was only a bad dream. Then she snapped to her senses. Midnight was hurt—she had to help him!

THOROUGHBRED

Ashleigh

GOOD-BYE, MIDNIGHT WANDERER

CREATED BY
JOANNA CAMPBELL

WRITTEN BY
OLIVIA COATES

HarperEntertainment
A Division of HarperCollinsPublishers

HarperEntertainment
A Division of HarperCollins*Publishers*
10 East 53rd Street, New York, NY 10022-5299

This is a work of fiction. The characters, incidents,
and dialogues are products of the author's imagination and are
not to be construed as real. Any resemblance to actual events or persons,
living or dead, is entirely coincidental.

Produced by 17th Street Productions,
a division of Daniel Weiss Associates, Inc.

ISBN 0–06–106557–9

Cover art © 1999 by Daniel Weiss Associates, Inc.

First printing: April 1999

Printed in the United States of America

Visit HarperEntertainment on the World Wide Web at
http://www.harpercollins.com

❖ 10 9 8 7 6 5 4 3 2 1

GOOD-BYE,
MIDNIGHT
WANDERER

"I'll race you to the barn, Caro!" Ashleigh Griffen called to her older sister, Caroline, as she dashed through the kitchen.

"But Ashleigh . . ." Caroline's voice trailed off as Ashleigh sprinted out the door.

It was Saturday—no school—and ten-year-old Ashleigh was in high spirits. She raced out of the little white farmhouse and turned the corner of the gravel path. Ahead of her, the big brown horse barn loomed, nestled amongst rolling Kentucky pastures. She stopped for a moment to catch her breath and gaze out over the white-fenced paddocks. Sleek Thoroughbreds grazed quietly, and an atmosphere of peacefulness filled the air. Ashleigh almost had to pinch herself to remember that Edgardale was home. *The most perfect home in the world,* Ashleigh thought. She drew her coat around her more tightly as a gust of icy wind made her shiver.

"Hi, Jonas," Ashleigh called across the barn to where

Edgardale's new stable manager was sweeping up.

"Morning," Jonas grunted in reply, his tall, gray-haired figure disappearing into the feed room before Ashleigh could strike up a conversation.

Ashleigh shrugged, grabbed a lead rope, and began to bring the horses out to the paddocks so that their stalls could be cleaned. Jonas was a funny sort of guy. He'd been at the farm only a few weeks—ever since their old stable manager, Kurt, had moved to Missouri to live on his sister's breeding farm. He was kind of unfriendly, but Ashleigh knew that didn't necessarily mean anything. Kurt hadn't been that welcoming when she'd first met him, and he'd gone on to become a really good friend.

Jonas had already given each horse its ration of grain, and now they were eagerly pulling hay from their hay nets while they waited to be led outside.

"That's enough of that, Georgie," Ashleigh murmured as the bay mare, My Georgina, went to take a bite out of her arm. She led the mare out the barn door and through the paddock gate, clipping it shut behind her. She hurried back for Stardust, her new riding horse. At the sound of Ashleigh's footfall, Stardust's chestnut head appeared over her door, and she nickered softly as Ashleigh rubbed the white stripe on her face.

Stardust was as good as gold as Ashleigh led her out to the paddock she shared with Moe, the Shetland pony that belonged to Ashleigh's six-year-old brother, Rory.

2

Midnight Wanderer was next. Back and forth Ashleigh and Jonas went with the different horses. When they were all out, exploring their paddocks and blinking in the early morning sunlight, Ashleigh returned to the barn to muck out the horses' stalls.

"Can I do Tonka's today?" Rory's little voice broke into Ashleigh's thoughts.

"I don't see why not." Ashleigh ruffled Rory's red-gold hair. "But don't forget you've got Moe's stall to do first—he's your number one priority now."

"How could I forget that, Ash?" Rory grinned.

Ashleigh smiled as Rory disappeared down the aisle. She knew her brother would be as good as his word. He adored the fuzzy-coated pony.

Ashleigh looked over her brother's shoulder to see her parents walking across the grass toward the barn. They were on their own. Maybe Caroline had swapped her stable chores for breakfast duties again that morning. Caroline always pitched in around the barn, but she really wasn't interested in horses. Ashleigh and Caroline were only three years apart in age, but the sisters couldn't have been more different.

Ashleigh got a wheelbarrow and pitchfork from the feed room and wheeled them to Stardust's stall. Next door, she could see Rory trying to fill a wheelbarrow with bedding. He was struggling, since the pitchfork was almost twice his height.

"Here, let me help," Ashleigh offered. Rory frowned, and Ashleigh immediately realized her mistake. Rory might be little, but he wanted to play as big a part in looking after the farm as she did. Ashleigh didn't say another word, and left him to it.

As soon as she had finished mucking out her stalls, Ashleigh started cleaning and filling up the water buckets. Then she set about sweeping the aisle.

When Ashleigh had swept up every stray bit of bedding, she went outside to watch the horses grazing peacefully on the patches of winter grass. The horses were all blanketed, but their necks shone in the sunlight. Gray horses, black horses, chestnut horses, bay horses—a complete host of colors.

The black colt, Midnight Wanderer, lifted his head and whinnied a greeting. Ashleigh smiled. He was the most valuable of this year's crop of yearlings, but that wasn't why she loved him so much. She loved him for his calm intelligence and gentle spirit. He'd inherited those qualities from his mother, Wanderer—Edgardale's prized broodmare. It was hard to believe that Midnight had once been the small foal Rory had nicknamed Tonka, after his favorite toy trucks. Now, with his muscled hindquarters and long straight legs, he looked every inch a racehorse in the making.

"I'm sorry, I haven't got anything for you," Ashleigh said as Midnight nuzzled her pockets for treats. She tickled his velvety nose. "But you've got all this nice grass."

Then Ashleigh remembered that some prospective buyers were coming to look at the yearlings that afternoon. They had heard about Midnight and had a particular interest in him. Ashleigh hated to admit it, but she didn't think Midnight would be at Edgardale for long, and of all the yearlings he was her favorite.

"I'm going to have to get going now," Ashleigh said, gently pushing Midnight's nose away. "I've got other jobs to do, and I'm going to ride Stardust, too."

Ashleigh's best friend, Mona Gardener, was bringing her bay Thoroughbred, Frisky, over so that they could go for a ride. The weather had been so bad lately, and the winter nights so long and cold, that they hadn't had a chance to go out together in a while. Ashleigh would have loved to stay with Midnight, but Stardust was badly in need of exercise.

She gave the colt one last pat and stood back to watch as Midnight shook his mane and galloped off to join the other yearlings. His gangly legs were a blur as he sped across the grass. He was fast—but with his bloodlines, that was hardly surprising. All of Wanderer's offspring were sound racehorses. Midnight's half-sister, Wanderer's Quest, had gone from strength to strength, winning stakes races in pretty tough company.

Ashleigh and her family had watched Wanderer's

Quest take second place in a graded stakes race at Churchill Downs. Now her owners were prepping her for the Florida Derby at Gulfstream Park—where the classy East Coast Thoroughbred scene went in the winter months. Although Ashleigh knew that Quest was likely to be the outsider of the field, she couldn't help harboring a secret hope that the mare would win. If Quest won that race, she'd be the most successful horse ever bred at Edgardale.

"With such an important mother and sister, you're going to be a real star," Ashleigh breathed as Midnight came to a halt in the paddock. He lifted his head, twitching his coal-black nostrils and looking in Ashleigh's direction.

"It'll be sad to see him go, won't it?" said a voice from behind her, disturbing her thoughts. Ashleigh spun around to find Jonas standing there.

"Yeah, really sad," Ashleigh agreed, surprised at Jonas's sudden show of emotion.

Jonas followed Ashleigh's line of vision to where Midnight stood grazing. "He sure is a game little colt. Your parents are expecting a good price for him."

"I know," Ashleigh replied with a nod. "If only we could keep him on the farm."

"What do you mean?" Jonas asked.

"Well . . ." Ashleigh hesitated. She would have told Kurt her dream any day, but with Jonas it was different.

6

How could she explain that she hoped her parents might keep Midnight on at Edgardale and train him themselves? It sounded silly, even to her own ears. Her parents didn't have the money for that, and even if they did, training yearlings to be great racehorses was something completely different from breeding them.

Ashleigh sighed. Keeping Midnight on the farm was just a dream. She had Stardust now. She should be concentrating on training her mare, not dreaming up ridiculous schemes.

"I'm going to take Stardust out now," Ashleigh said, sweeping back her long dark hair and grabbing a lead shank from the fence. She hurried across the grass to where Stardust was grazing quietly. The copper-colored mare looked up as Ashleigh approached, her ears twitching back and forth.

"Hey there," Ashleigh murmured. Stardust had been on the farm only a few weeks, and they were still getting to know each other. The part-Thoroughbred had been roughly handled before arriving at Edgardale—and by a girl of about Ashleigh's age and size—so Ashleigh was having a difficult time winning Stardust's confidence.

"Easy does it," Ashleigh breathed, ready for any trick the mare might pull. But Stardust seemed to relax, and Ashleigh clipped the lead shank onto her halter with ease.

"You see, that wasn't so bad, was it?" Ashleigh patted

Stardust's sleek neck, leading her off across the grass and into the barn.

It was quiet inside and would stay that way until the afternoon, when the horses were brought in for the night. As Ashleigh walked up the center aisle, the warm scent of hay surrounded her. There were twenty-four roomy box stalls in the barn, twelve on each side of the aisle. With ten broodmares and ten yearlings to house, the farm was pretty full at the moment. But it wouldn't be like that for long. Starting that day, more and more private buyers would be coming to look at the yearlings. Any that weren't sold that way would go to the Keeneland yearling auction in the fall. Again, Ashleigh felt sad at the thought of saying good-bye to the babies they'd bred and nurtured over the last year. But it was how the farm survived, and what paid for the upkeep of next year's foals.

Once Stardust was safely in her stall, Ashleigh went to look for her parents. Mrs. Griffen was in the office, her blond head bent over the feeding charts. Both Rory and Caroline were fair-haired, like their mother, while Ashleigh took after her dark-haired father.

"Mom, I've mucked out my stalls and filled up all the water buckets. Mona's coming over soon to ride. Is it okay if I get Stardust ready?"

"Yes, that's fine," her mother answered. "I know you need the practice."

"Thanks, Mom," Ashleigh said, frowning. She knew her mother meant her words kindly, but Ashleigh didn't like to be reminded that she still had a lot of work to put in with Stardust. She and the mare had come a long way, but in the early days, Ashleigh had spent more time on the ground than in the saddle. Her parents had wondered if Stardust wasn't too much for Ashleigh to handle. They had even suggested returning the mare to her original owners, but Ashleigh had begged them to give her time. She became determined to get along with Stardust, and once her father showed her some helpful training techniques, Stardust began to trust Ashleigh more and more. Her parents had finally agreed to keep Stardust at Edgardale, but Ashleigh was always worried they might change their minds if Stardust tried anything risky. She just couldn't let that happen.

Ashleigh gathered her tack and put the chestnut mare in crossties in the aisle.

"Now, no messing around today. Right, Stardust?" she said as she lifted the saddle up onto the mare's back.

Stardust pawed at the ground, as if in response, and Ashleigh patted her neck to soothe her. Stardust was certainly more playful than usual—they'd have to get going quickly. Gently Ashleigh fed the bit into the mare's mouth and drew the bridle up over her head before fastening the throatlatch. Then she tightened the girth once more. They were ready. As Ashleigh led Stardust out of the barn, she looked up at the sky. It was a clear, brisk day, perfect for riding. Ashleigh walked Stardust up the drive and was relieved to see that Mona had arrived, leading Frisky.

Ashleigh waved to her friend. "Whoa, Stardust," she called as Stardust skittered forward.

"Hi, Ashleigh," Mona called, pushing her curly dark hair out of her eyes. "I think Frisky's got a stone in her shoe. I'm just going to take her in the barn and pick it out. I'll meet you by the paddocks."

"Okay," Ashleigh agreed as she sprang up into Stardust's saddle and squeezed her legs, keen to keep her horse moving. But Stardust dug her hooves in, refusing to walk forward.

"You're all right, you'll be fine," Ashleigh coaxed, scratching Stardust's withers. But the mare was acting unhappier by the minute. It wasn't until Ashleigh jumped down off her back and led her onto the grass that she would go forward into the paddock lanes.

"There's no one there—it's just you and me. Hold still." Ashleigh hopped around with her left foot in the stirrup as she tried to mount up. The chestnut mare shook her red-brown mane as Ashleigh settled down into the saddle.

"Come on, Mona, hurry up," she said under her breath.

Ashleigh twisted around and frowned as she caught

sight of her parents watching from the patch of grass by the barn. That was all she needed—for them to see Stardust acting up again. Ashleigh felt ill at ease. It was cold out, but her hands were hot and sticky.

"Mona, where are you?" Ashleigh shouted. Then she breathed a sigh of relief as she saw Mona and Frisky coming across the grass at a collected trot. Mona had had Frisky only since Christmas, but they went together like a dream. *Like you and I are going to,* Ashleigh thought as she leaned down to pat Stardust's neck.

"I got the stone out," Mona said, waving her crop. "All set?"

"Put that down, please, Mona," Ashleigh called, feeling Stardust tense beneath her.

"Sorry," Mona apologized. "Stardust looks like she's feeling fresh."

"We'll be all right once we get going," Ashleigh said firmly, nudging Stardust forward. "We have to be back by three, though. There are some people coming to look at Midnight."

"Okay, Ash," Mona assured her. "Let's go!"

As she settled down into Stardust's saddle, Ashleigh fully expected the mare to bolt forward. But Stardust remained perfectly calm. Ashleigh clucked her on and they trotted off down the paddock lanes, with Mona and Frisky in stride beside them.

Once they had gone a little way, Ashleigh's hands

didn't feel quite so shaky and she calmed down, breathing deeply.

"You and Stardust look good today," Mona remarked.

"Yeah, I guess she can behave herself when she wants to," Ashleigh said with a laugh, looking over at Frisky and Mona. Frisky trotted calmly at Mona's request. They seemed to be made for each other.

Stardust and Frisky trotted along side by side, winding their way uphill, their breath floating up in frosty white clouds. It was a crisp, bright winter day, Stardust was behaving herself, and Ashleigh began to relax and enjoy the ride.

When they had ridden a little way up into the hills, Ashleigh and Mona halted their horses and turned back to look at the farm below them. It looked smaller, but they could still see everything clearly.

"Look, there's Mom and Dad and Jonas over by the barn," Ashleigh said, pointing.

"I see them. Hey, can you tell from here which yearling is which?" Mona asked.

"Of course," Ashleigh said. "There's Sparky, and Pip, and Tip, and Dollar, and Rosie, and there's Midnight, my favorite. You know, we've broken them all to halter and lead line now, but some of them are still kind of jumpy. Mom and Dad are going to be working with them this afternoon. We could help if you want to," she offered.

"Really? That would be great," Mona agreed.

The two girls rode on in companionable silence. Ashleigh was pleased that things were back on an even keel. She and Mona had argued over just about everything at Christmastime. Ashleigh knew it had been mostly her fault. She'd been pretty touchy about Stardust in the beginning. Every little suggestion Mona had made had seemed like a personal criticism.

"I think we're going to have to ride single file," Ashleigh said, nodding ahead of her as the path narrowed and they wound their way farther uphill.

"This is the path we started out on when we found Lightning, isn't it?" Mona reminded her.

Ashleigh thought about the white mare they'd found on the ramshackle farm on the other side of the woods. Lightning had been living in squalor back then. She'd been as thin as a rake and very depressed, but thanks to Kurt they'd managed to get her back to Edgardale, and Ashleigh had nursed her back to health. For a while Ashleigh had thought of Lightning as her own horse. Parting with her had been extremely difficult.

Ashleigh had given the mare to the Hopewell Center at Christmastime. The center treated children with cancer, and used animals for therapy. They'd needed a horse and wanted to adopt Lightning. When Ashleigh had met the patients and staff at the center and seen the love they had to give, she knew that Lightning could ask for no better home.

Ashleigh was quiet, thinking, as Stardust picked her way along the trail.

"Have you heard from Kira at all?" Mona asked. Kira was a Hopewell patient who'd ridden and looked after Lightning at the center. She'd become a good friend of Ashleigh and Mona's, but when her condition had improved Kira had moved back to Ohio to live with her parents.

"I got a letter from her last week," Ashleigh said, and wrinkled her forehead. "She wanted to know how Lightning was. I can't really tell her till I've been to Hopewell—but I've been putting it off. After all the trouble I've been having with Stardust, I know seeing Lightning will just make me sad."

"Yeah, but you and Stardust are going to be fine from now on. She looks great," Mona assured her. "Hey, I can see the spring ahead of us. Let's canter!"

"Okay," Ashleigh called. She nudged Stardust on and chased Mona and Frisky across the mossy path to the spring.

"Lunch stop?" Ashleigh suggested, pulling up to a halt as they reached the muddy banks of the spring. Mona nodded eagerly.

Jumping to the ground, the two girls tied their horses and spread out their parkas to sit down on. Happily they munched away on the sandwiches, potato chips, and chocolate Mona had brought with her. Stardust tried to pick up the piece of plastic wrap the sandwiches had been wrapped in, nibbling at it and pushing it across the ground. Ashleigh only just managed to grab it in time.

"Hey, silly girl. That won't taste good," Ashleigh said with a chuckle.

"Boy, it could have been nasty if she'd swallowed that," Mona said. "But she's so much fun, Ash. What a clown."

Ashleigh hadn't ever thought of Stardust that way, but Mona was right—Stardust could be pretty funny sometimes. Ashleigh was happy their ride was going so well. Maybe all the trouble with Stardust was behind her.

Soon the girls had finished their food. "It's getting late. Should we head back down?" Ashleigh suggested, remembering the buyers who were coming to look at Midnight. She didn't want to miss them.

"Sure, and when we get back to your house let's make some hot chocolate to warm up," Mona said.

"Okay," Ashleigh agreed. Quickly the two girls got to their feet and remounted. As they rode back down the path they'd come from, they found it easy to find their way—the ground was soft underfoot, and the horses' hoofprints were clearly visible. Ashleigh leaned back and rested her hand on Stardust's backside to take the weight off the mare's forelegs.

"Take it easy, it's slippery up here," Ashleigh called back to her friend. "Follow me. This path is less steep."

As they followed the path downhill and got nearer to Edgardale, Ashleigh and Mona could see the farm clearly now—the horse barn lay ahead of them, and a thin wisp of smoke spiraled up into the air above the house. Ashleigh smiled at the thought of warming herself by the fire inside.

"Brrr! Come on, Mona," Ashleigh said, trotting Stardust into the canopy of trees. As they rode out the other side, Ashleigh looked down at Edgardale.

"What's going on down there?" Mona pointed to a group of people gathered by the paddocks and a strange car parked by the house. It looked as though the prospective buyers were already there.

"They must have come early." Ashleigh frowned. "Let's go!"

The yearlings looked up with interest as the two girls trotted along the grassy lane between the paddocks. Ashleigh could see her parents talking to a man and a woman. Jonas walked out into the paddocks and clipped a lead shank onto Midnight Wanderer's halter.

Ashleigh tried to look nonchalant as she and Mona rode up alongside the fence and jumped to the ground.

"Hi, Ashleigh. Hi, Mona," Mrs. Griffen called. "We were wondering when you two might get back." She turned to their guests. "This is our daughter, Ashleigh, and her friend, Mona," she said, introducing the two girls.

"And this is Mr. and Mrs. Finch-Brown." Mr. Griffen indicated the blond woman at his side, and her burly husband. "They own Stony Brooks Farm."

"I was just telling them how you've looked after Midnight since he was a foal," Mrs. Griffen said.

"A real family enterprise you've got going here," Mr. Finch-Brown commented with a smile. Then he asked Ashleigh, "So he's an easygoing colt, is he? Good temperament?"

"Um . . . yes, he is." Ashleigh stumbled over the words. She didn't want to make Midnight sound too good, or they'd take him. Yet at the same time, she couldn't sell him short. Midnight had never given her a moment's trouble. He was so sweet and good-natured.

"He's certainly got good bloodlines. We saw Wanderer's Quest run at Gulfstream a couple of weeks back," Mrs. Finch-Brown explained. "She ran a good, solid race. If this colt's got her staying power, he'll make a wonderful miler."

Stardust was getting restless just standing there, but Ashleigh's eyes were fixed on Midnight as Jonas led him around the paddock. His ears were pricked and his eyes sparkled. Her parents had removed his blanket so that the Finch-Browns could get a good look. Newly developed muscles rippled beneath his black coat as he danced merrily on his toes. He was so beautiful—the complete picture of health. Ashleigh bit her bottom lip. They'd want him, she just knew it. Why would they pick any of the other yearlings? Midnight was the best of them all.

The couple walked a little ways away, and looked as though they were conferring, glancing every now and then back into the paddock. They were probably deciding on a price to offer.

"All right, Jonas. You can let him off that lead line now," Mr. Griffen called.

Ashleigh felt a lump rising in her throat. She saw her mother look anxiously to where the couple was still huddled, talking. It was hardly surprising her parents were taking this so seriously. If they could sell Midnight so early on, it would be a fantastic start to the season.

"I guess I'd better go home," Mona said, leading Frisky alongside Stardust. She touched Ashleigh's elbow. "Are you all right?"

"I'm sorry, Mona. I'm just sad about Midnight being sold, that's all," Ashleigh admitted. "I know I said we could help Jonas with the babies, but maybe some other time, okay?"

"We had a great ride, though," Mona reminded her. "Let's go again soon."

Ashleigh nodded. Mona was right. Stardust had gone perfectly for her and they'd had a terrific time. Until now. "I'll call you later and let you know what happens," Ashleigh added, gesturing toward the Finch-Browns.

After Mona left, Ashleigh led Stardust into the barn. Caroline was there, refilling the hay nets.

"What's with the mood, Ash? You look like someone died," Caroline said when she saw her. Ashleigh groaned. Her sister's sarcasm was the last thing she needed.

"It's just those people, the Finch-Browns," Ashleigh explained as she untacked Stardust and led her into her stall.

"Have they picked one yet?" Caroline went on. "They seemed really interested."

"What do you care, anyway?" Ashleigh demanded. As soon as the words were out of her mouth, she was sorry she'd said them. It *was* a family business, as Mr. Finch-Brown had commented, and even though Caroline wasn't as interested in horses as Ashleigh was, Ashleigh knew her sister wanted the farm to succeed.

"You're not upset, are you?" Caroline asked with a shrewd look at her younger sister. "It's not a good idea to get too attached to the yearlings. I thought you'd grown out of that."

"I know," Ashleigh muttered, pushing past her sister and walking out toward the paddocks again.

"Ashleigh, are you okay?" Caroline called, following her.

"Yes, I'm fine," Ashleigh answered, though she didn't

feel fine at all. Why should these people have Midnight? It wasn't fair. She was the one who had looked after him when he was small—loved him, cared for him. But at the same time she knew she was being selfish. If Stony Brooks was a big farm, then Midnight would get the best training possible. He could become the champion he was meant to be. And if that happened, word would spread about the quality horses Edgardale bred, and the farm could grow, too.

"Look, they're coming back over. They must have made a decision," Caroline whispered. Ashleigh turned back to listen.

"Well, I have to say we're pretty impressed," Mr. Finch-Brown began. "He's a magnificent animal."

"Why don't we go into the house and talk?" Mr. Griffen said.

Ashleigh's heart sank. The deal was as good as done. She turned away and looked sadly out into the paddocks. Midnight was there, trotting merrily along the fence. Ashleigh's heart ached. He was so beautiful. All she could hope for was that the Finch-Browns wouldn't want to take him back to their farm right away. Her eyes darted over to the far corner, where a group of yearlings were teasing each other into play. One of the little fillies kicked up her heels and galloped off, setting a blazing trail across the paddocks. The others were in hot pursuit.

"I know it's hard, Ash," Caroline went on, "but—"

"Quiet," Ashleigh shushed her as Midnight trotted across the paddock. He was heading toward Sparky, the most rambunctious of the yearlings and a trouble-maker. Sparky's neck was already arched defiantly, as if he was bracing for a fight, and he let loose with a series of bucks as Midnight drew closer. The black colt did a sideways jump, flicking his tail in annoyance.

"Uh-oh," Caroline murmured. "It looks like they're going to fight." She turned around, looking for their parents. Mr. and Mrs. Griffen were deep in conversation with the Finch-Browns and were just about to enter the house. "I'll run over there and get them."

"No, you don't have to do that," Ashleigh insisted. "Remember when Slammer used to round up the other yearlings and boss them around like he was the stud of the herd? I wanted him to go in his own paddock so he would leave them alone, but Mom and Dad said we shouldn't try to tame his spirit," she explained. "They told me it was natural for horses to fight with each other—it's what gives them the edge to win on the track."

"Well, if you say so . . . you're the horse expert, not me," Caroline said with a resigned shrug, but she looked worried.

The sisters watched in silence. Midnight pawed the earth like a bull, and Sparky shook his head, his eyes rolling.

"Come on, Ash," Caroline said, tugging on Ashleigh's sleeve. "Let's go hear what's going on." She gestured back to the couple from Stony Brooks. "It looks like they're going to make a deal."

"In a minute," Ashleigh said. She wanted to watch what was happening in the paddock. The two young horses were staring each other down now. Ashleigh's eyes were trained on Midnight.

"Come on, boy," she muttered under her breath. "Show him who's boss."

The yearlings pawed at the ground. Their tails twitched angrily as they kicked up the turf. Then suddenly they were up on their muscled, powerful hind legs, locked in battle. Midnight's nostrils were blood red, and his forelegs flailed as he fought for control.

Which one will give in first? Ashleigh's eyes narrowed. "You can do it, Midnight," she urged as Midnight and Sparky touched down, and then rose up again. Sparky made a lunge for Midnight's shoulder, and Midnight twisted in midair as he tried to avoid Sparky's gnashing teeth.

Ashleigh glanced back at her parents to see if they were watching, but they were still talking with the Finch-Browns just outside the house.

Suddenly there was a sickening, splintering crunch, and Ashleigh whipped her head around to see Midnight toppling over backward. Sparky backed away as the black horse flailed on his back for a moment, whinnying hysterically. Ashleigh couldn't believe her ears. The screeching, high-pitched whinny that rose and filled the air was like nothing she'd ever heard before. Finally Midnight scrambled to his feet, reeling sideways and teetering painfully on three legs. His right hind leg was hovering above the ground.

Ashleigh felt sick to the bottom of her stomach, frozen to the spot. *It's Midnight's leg—he's hurt it badly*, she thought, hoping it was only a bad dream. Then she snapped to her senses. Midnight was hurt—she had to help him!

"Midnight!" she screamed. And before anyone could stop her, Ashleigh vaulted over the gate and ran across the grass at full speed.

2

As Ashleigh ran, she had no thought as to what she would do or the danger she might be in. She heard Caroline cry out behind her, but even then she didn't stop. She sprinted across the field, drawing to a halt when she was just in front of the panic-stricken horse. Midnight looked at her with trusting eyes. He was depending on her for help, but Ashleigh didn't know what to do. She was afraid to get too close, in case Midnight spooked and tried to run, hurting himself even more. Ashleigh looked back across the paddock. There was no one in sight.

Midnight's hysterical whinnies seemed to cry, *What's happening to me?* Despite his injured leg, he was still trying to walk. With every step he tried to take, the pain was clearly reflected in his eyes.

"Easy, boy," Ashleigh called. "You're going to be all right."

Suddenly Jonas was at her side. It had been only seconds since Midnight's fall, but it had seemed like an eternity. Ashleigh breathed a sigh of relief. At least someone was there to help.

Jonas was edging closer and closer now, trying to reach for the colt's head.

"Easy does it, Midnight. Easy," Jonas crooned. The black horse eyed him warily.

Jonas took one more step and reached forward, grabbing hold of the yearling's halter and clipping a lead shank on it. Midnight yanked his head up, his eyes showing their whites.

"I've got you. Easy, boy," Jonas said in a soothing voice, rubbing Midnight's nose. With a quick glance back at Ashleigh, he said, "Can you talk to him?"

Ashleigh felt the stickiness of her palms as she held out her hand and approached the suffering horse. "There, Midnight, there," Ashleigh breathed. She felt dizzy as she looked at his injured leg, hanging limply. Behind them there was a rustle of grass. Ashleigh turned to see her father running toward them with a bucket of supplies in his hand. When he was within a few yards of them, he slowed down.

"Caroline told me what happened," he said breathlessly. "I went back to get the bute and the ace from the barn," he explained grimly. "The ace will keep him calm for a while. Try to keep him still, Jonas," he ordered.

Ace—acepromazine—was a tranquilizer. Bute—

phenylbutazone—was for the pain. In Midnight's state, they'd need to give him both just to get the horse safely to his stall.

Midnight tried to kick out with his good hind leg and nearly fell over, but Mr. Griffen managed to get the first shot in his neck.

"Is he going to be all right?" Ashleigh asked desperately.

Her father looked away. "We've called Dr. Frankel. He's on his way."

Ashleigh knew from the grimace on her father's face that things were pretty bad. Still, Dr. Frankel was a brilliant horse vet—the best in the area. He'd know what to do. Ashleigh stroked Midnight's neck, trying to soothe him, but she couldn't bring herself to look at his injured leg.

"We've got to get him back to the barn," Mr. Griffen said. "Your mother's driving the trailer over, but I want to wrap his leg first. We need to keep it stable so he doesn't injure it any more."

Jonas and Ashleigh stood at Midnight's head while Mr. Griffen crouched down and carefully wound a padded cotton bandage around the leg. Midnight flinched but stood still. Then, starting at the pastern and going up to the hock, Mr. Griffen covered the cotton bandage with an elasticized wrap, finishing off with tape to hold it in place.

"There, it's all done," Ashleigh crooned, rubbing the black yearling's forehead.

"You go back to the house, Ashleigh," Mr. Griffen said, standing up. "You won't want to see this."

"Please, Dad," Ashleigh begged. "I want to be with Midnight. I have to know what's going to happen to him. And besides, I bet he'll go into the trailer for me."

Ashleigh's father didn't argue with her. Ashleigh had a knack with the young horses, and Midnight had been in a trailer only a few times.

The trailer was making slow progress toward them, backing to a standstill about twenty yards away. Ashleigh's mother jumped out, and Jonas helped her put the ramp down. Midnight's brown eyes bulged in terror, and he tried to hop away.

"It's all right, sweetie. It's going to be all right," Ashleigh whispered desperately.

"We have to get him up there," Mr. Griffen said. He wound the lead shank through the halter and behind Midnight's ears. "This might work better. Ashleigh, take his head. I'll get behind him."

Ashleigh picked up the lead. *Will Midnight go forward on three legs? Can he still feel the pain through the bute?* she wondered.

"Come on, boy. Do it for me," Ashleigh said under her breath.

Her eyes never left Midnight as she led the young horse forward, talking to him all the time. The tranquilizer was really taking effect now. Midnight's head had dropped and the wildness had gone out of his eyes. Through sheer willpower, Midnight hobbled up the ramp after Ashleigh and into the horse trailer. Ashleigh clipped the trailer tie to the side of his halter. Her parents' anxious faces peered in at her.

"I'll stay with him in the back. You go in the cab, Ashleigh," her father called.

"I want to stay here," Ashleigh protested. "He's calmer now. He won't strike out."

"Then I'll come with you," her father said.

There was no time to argue. Mrs. Griffen and Jonas put up the ramp, and they set off. As they drove across the paddocks Ashleigh rubbed Midnight's nose, avoiding her father's pained gaze.

"We'll be there soon, boy." Ashleigh patted Midnight's shoulder as they pulled in front of the barn door. Rory and Caroline's faces were the first things that Ashleigh saw as the ramp came down. She could hardly bear to look at Caroline. After all, Caroline had been right. Why hadn't Ashleigh listened to her and stopped the yearlings from fighting? Ashleigh felt terrible. This was all her fault.

Slowly Midnight backed out of the trailer, and Ashleigh led him into the nearest stall. The poor colt could barely put any weight on the toe of his back right foot. Every step took a huge effort.

Mr. Griffen glanced at his watch. "Dr. Frankel will be here any minute," he said as they all crowded around.

Ashleigh nodded, trying to stifle the choking feeling that was rising in her throat.

A Bronco drew up and Dr. Frankel jumped out. He walked straight over to the stall, acknowledging the Griffens with a nod.

"Caroline, Ashleigh, take Rory back to the house," Mr. Griffen ordered.

"Can't I stay?" Ashleigh pleaded.

"Please, Ashleigh," Mr. Griffen insisted. "I'll tell you everything once we know how bad his injury is, but having everyone hanging around isn't going to help Midnight."

Ashleigh knew her father was right, so she followed Caroline away from the barn and into the house, leading Rory by the hand. Her mind was whirring. Leg injuries were difficult to fix in horses, especially high-strung ones such as Thoroughbreds. It was so hard to immobilize them. If the bone was broken, the horse often had to be destroyed.

"Is Tonka hurt bad?" Rory asked, standing by Ashleigh's side as she sat down at the kitchen table to wait. His face was streaked with tears. "Will he be okay?"

Caroline opened the refrigerator and shot Ashleigh a warning glance.

"Oh, Rory," Ashleigh said, and hugged him close. It was bad enough for Ashleigh and Caroline to see Midnight hurt so seriously, but Rory was too small to understand.

"Don't worry," she said, trying to reassure herself as well as her brother. "I'm sure things will be all right." She squeezed Rory tight. "Right, Caro?"

"Right," Caroline said, pulling up a chair. But she didn't sound convinced.

Over Rory's shoulder, Ashleigh peered out of the kitchen window. She couldn't see anything. Everyone was still in the barn.

"Do you want to hold my Tonka truck?" Rory offered. He pulled away, picking up his truck from the floor and handing it to Ashleigh.

"Thank you," Ashleigh said absentmindedly, taking the little red truck and turning it over and over in her hands.

Dr. Frankel seemed to be taking forever. Ashleigh stood up and paced in front of the window. Finally she could take it no longer. She made a dash for the door. Rory was right behind her.

"Ashleigh, wait!" Caroline called. "Mom and Dad said to wait till the vet leaves."

Caroline's words followed her, but Ashleigh wasn't listening. She looked behind her and realized that Rory had followed her outside. Dr. Frankel and her parents were standing in the barn doorway. Ashleigh could hear some of the words: ". . . since it's the cannon bone, there's not much chance . . ." Ashleigh's heart began to beat faster.

"Could you go and find me the blue truck? That's my favorite one," she said to Rory, eager to send him away so that he couldn't hear what the vet was saying.

"Sure, Ash," Rory said, looking surprised. "I'll be back in a minute."

As Rory disappeared into the house, Ashleigh made her way over to where her parents were huddled with Dr. Frankel. All three met her gaze, their faces creased with worry.

"Midnight's leg is broken and he's in a lot of pain," Dr. Frankel explained. "As you know, a cannon bone fracture is the hardest break to fix. He'll certainly never be able to race."

Ashleigh looked up at the vet, her eyes brimming over with tears of disbelief. Even though she had been worried about Midnight, she hadn't really been prepared for this. *A broken leg? It can't be. Not Midnight. He's too special. He's our best yearling—he* has *to race!* she thought, desperate to reassure herself.

"I'm sorry, Ashleigh," Dr. Frankel said. "I know you care for Midnight. But your parents have to make some important decisions now."

"Important decisions?" Ashleigh demanded, confused. "What do you mean?"

"Well," Dr. Frankel said, "he'll certainly never run, and even if the fracture does heal enough for him to be a pleasure horse or to keep at stud, he'll probably have to be on a lot of medication for the rest of his life. He'll never pass a vet's examination, so he'll be unlikely to get a buyer. He'd be a very expensive horse to keep up. It's a shame—he looks like a promising animal—but for the pain he's going to be in, I think it would be best to put him down."

"*No!*" Ashleigh's shout startled everyone, including herself. She couldn't let this happen. There just had to be another way.

"Mom, Dad, you can't put Midnight down," she pleaded, looking from her mother to her father. "Even if he can't ever race, we could get his leg to heal so we can trail-ride him. And we could use him for stud, right?" Her words tumbled out in a rush. "At least give him a chance?"

Mrs. Griffen took a deep breath and turned back to the vet. "What chance is there of the leg healing so he's comfortable?"

"It's very slim, Elaine," Dr. Frankel said grimly. "He'd need an immobilizing cast, and complete stall rest. The healing power in his young bones is to his advantage, but it'll be nearly impossible to keep such a young horse so still."

"We could at least try," Ashleigh interrupted. "I'll look after him."

"He'll be in a lot of pain in the early stages," Dr. Frankel told them.

"What if we gave him painkillers?" Mr. Griffen asked.

"You'd have to," the vet said thoughtfully. "He'd need steroids to bring the swelling down, and at least two hefty shots of painkillers a day on top of that—bute would do the trick. I can prescribe some antibiotics to prevent infection, too. And if you're serious about this, you'd have to have plenty of acepromazine around to tranquilize him—he may get hard to handle and end up harming himself even more."

Mr. Griffen nodded thoughtfully and looked over at Ashleigh's mother, who was standing with her arms crossed and a frown on her face.

"It might get better," Ashleigh said, trying to sound determined. Her parents looked unsure.

"At least give him a little time," Ashleigh begged. "Let's try."

Dr. Frankel stood patiently, waiting for a decision.

"Please," Ashleigh tried again. "He's an Edgardale foal, our foal," she said, playing on her parents' weakness, knowing that neither of them would want to give up on a horse they'd bred themselves, especially not one of Wanderer's foals.

Ashleigh's mother and father looked at each other for

33

a few moments. Then Mr. Griffen finally let out a deep sigh. "All right, this is what I propose. My head tells me to put him out of his misery now, but my heart tells me to give him a chance. He adores Ashleigh, and she might be able to keep him quiet. Let's put him in a cast, and we'll see how he's doing in two weeks. If the bone hasn't started to knit, then of course we'll have to do the kindest thing. Elaine, what do you think?"

Mrs. Griffen brushed a few strands of hair off her forehead. She looked tired. "I agree. Let's see how it goes."

"Thank you! Oh, thank you!" Ashleigh exclaimed in relief, hugging first her father, then her mother.

"I don't want you getting your hopes up," Mrs. Griffen warned her daughter. "This isn't going to be easy."

"I won't, I won't," Ashleigh promised, but plans were already spinning around in her head. She'd sit with Midnight night and day. She'd talk to him. She'd read to him. She'd get him to rest. She just had to make him well again. They couldn't put Midnight down. Not now, not ever!

The vet turned to Mr. Griffen. "Well, if that's what you've decided, then let's get that cast on Midnight right now, while he's still calm."

Mr. Griffen nodded. "Then we'll go discuss what drugs and supplies we'll need for the next couple of weeks, while we see how the injury is healing." He looked at Ashleigh. "I need you to go help Jonas with the other horses now. Your mother has to go talk to the Finch-Browns—they're still waiting in the office. They won't buy Midnight now, of course, but they seemed to like a couple of the other yearlings, too."

Ashleigh said nothing.

Her father sighed again and looked toward the barn. "I don't think Midnight's going to like this cast business one bit."

It was dark in the barn as Ashleigh stood in Midnight's stall that evening. The black colt was quiet now, and he leaned into her, nuzzling her shoulder.

"My poor, poor Midnight," Ashleigh crooned, pressing her cheek against his soft black one.

The night had crept in without Ashleigh noticing, and she was tired. But she didn't care—Midnight needed her. She looked at the white cast on the colt's hind leg. It stretched all the way from his hoof to the tip of his hock. The vet had shaved the leg, and around the edges of the cast, by the point of the hock, Midnight's dark skin was already chafed from rubbing against the plaster. The yearling had had so much medication pumped into him that the life had gone out of his expression. It was as though he had grown old in just a few hours.

"It's all my fault, Midnight," Ashleigh berated herself. "I should have stopped you and Sparky in the paddocks when I could. Oh, why didn't I?"

"What was that, Ash?" The voice behind Ashleigh made her jump. It was Caroline.

"Nothing," Ashleigh said.

"Are you going to come get some dinner?" Caroline suggested. "Mom thinks you should eat something."

"I'm not hungry," Ashleigh insisted, clutching her elbows and shivering in the cold night air.

"You can't stay out here all night," Caroline coaxed.

"I have to. Midnight needs me," Ashleigh answered.

"Not as much as Mom and Dad need your support right now," Caroline said sensibly. "They're pretty upset, too. I mean, the vet said the leg might heal, but Midnight's racing career is over. They'll never be able to sell him, and he was the most valuable yearling we had. They've lost a lot of money because of this."

"How can you talk about money at a time like this?" Ashleigh cried.

Caroline shrugged, but there was a sympathetic look in her eyes. "I know it's hard to think about anything else when Midnight's hurt so badly, but you know the money from the sale of the yearlings is what keeps this farm going—it pays for our food and clothes, for Stardust and Moe's food, for—"

"Stardust!" Ashleigh spun around. "I haven't groomed

or fed her!" With everything that had happened, Ashleigh had forgotten all about her mare.

"It's all right. I did it for you."

"You did?" Ashleigh looked at her sister in disbelief.

"Well, somebody had to," Caroline said, and shrugged. "If you're staying out here, I'm going back to the house."

"No, wait," Ashleigh said. "I'll come with you."

Caroline stood back from Midnight's stall, waiting for Ashleigh to join her.

Ashleigh hugged the colt one more time before saying good night. He was so drugged up, he hardly even noticed her.

"Oh, Midnight," Ashleigh whispered, the tears sliding down her cheeks. "I know I wanted you to stay at Edgardale, but not like this. Not this way."

It was well past the Griffens' usual dinner hour. Ashleigh was exhausted and she didn't feel like eating, but she knew she had to sit down with her family. There was an uncomfortable silence in the kitchen as Caroline held the plates for Mrs. Griffen to spoon out the macaroni and cheese. Rory kicked at the legs of his chair. Ashleigh couldn't bear to look at his tearstained face.

Mrs. Griffen turned the stove off and sat down at the table. "I know no one wants to talk about the accident right now, but I have to know—did anyone actually see how it started?"

"I was so busy talking to the Finch-Browns that I wasn't watching the paddocks," Mr. Griffen explained.

"I didn't really see anything," Caroline said quickly, pushing her food around her plate. She didn't look at Ashleigh.

Ashleigh looked across the table at her sister. She'd expected Caroline to tell their parents that Ashleigh had told her to leave the horses alone even though Caroline had wanted to go get help. But Caroline didn't say a word. She was obviously covering for Ashleigh.

Ashleigh put her head down, staring at her plate.

"Ashleigh, are you all right?" Mrs. Griffen asked. "I know this was a nasty shock for you—it was for all of us."

Ashleigh nodded. Her mouth felt dry. She pushed her plate away and slid her chair back from the table.

"Can I go to bed now?" she asked, getting to her feet.

"Oh, Ashleigh, you've got to eat," Mrs. Griffen groaned.

"Let her go," Mr. Griffen said, and laid a hand on his wife's arm. "If she's not hungry, she's not hungry."

"Good night, everyone," Ashleigh mumbled, walking into the hallway. She dragged herself upstairs and made her way into the bedroom she shared with Caroline. Prince Charming, the Maine Coon kitten she'd gotten for Christmas, was curled up on her quilt, fast asleep. Ashleigh left him alone and got ready for bed.

As she brushed her teeth Ashleigh stared at the little china horses on the bathroom windowsill, seeing them but not seeing them. She flicked off the bathroom light and headed back to her bedroom. Nudging her kitten over, Ashleigh got into bed and lay back in the darkness. Prince Charming stretched and rearranged himself at her side.

A moment later Caroline pushed open the door of their bedroom.

"Ash," Caroline whispered, "you awake?"

Ashleigh didn't answer, and she squeezed her eyes tightly shut as Caroline switched on her bedside light.

"I know you're awake," Caroline said quietly as she began to change for bed. "I hope you won't go blaming yourself for what happened out there today. It wasn't your fault. It was an accident. You couldn't have known how it was going to turn out."

Caroline went into the bathroom to brush her teeth. Ashleigh lay with her eyes closed, thinking about what Caroline had said. Despite their differences, Ashleigh knew that Caroline cared about her, and she knew that her sister hated seeing her so miserable.

"Accidents do happen," Caroline said, coming back into the room and turning off the light. "I just don't want you to think Midnight's leg is your fault, Ashleigh," she continued as she got into bed. "You do so much for those horses."

A tear rolled down Ashleigh's cheek. Caroline's kind words made her feel even worse, because she knew deep down that she *was* at least partly responsible for Midnight's suffering.

"Good night, Caro," Ashleigh said in a quiet voice. "Thanks."

"Mmm." Soon Ashleigh heard Caroline's breathing become slow and regular as she dozed off into sleep.

Ashleigh opened her eyes and stared at the ceiling as she replayed the accident over and over in her mind. *If only I'd shouted for the horses to stop . . . if only I'd let Caro call Mom and Dad . . . if only . . .* Eventually she started to feel sleepy and her eyes began to close. Her last thought was: *Two weeks until the vet comes back. I've got two weeks to get Midnight better.*

3

The piercing beep of the alarm clock was the first thing Ashleigh heard the next morning. She fumbled around for the switch and looked across the room at Caroline. Her sister stirred but remained asleep. Ashleigh slipped out of bed and scrambled into her clothes. The house was quiet as she headed out to the barn.

Some of the horses were out grazing in the paddocks, and when Ashleigh arrived, Jonas was busy mucking out their stalls.

"How's Midnight?" Ashleigh asked right away.

"He isn't on his feet yet. It looks like he's hurting," Jonas said. "I already gave him a shot of bute."

Just at that moment Ashleigh heard a pitiful nicker coming from Midnight's stall. She rushed down the aisle and looked in over his door. Midnight was lying completely still in the straw. If Ashleigh hadn't heard his cry, she would have sworn he was asleep. Her heart went out to him when she saw his cast, stretched out awkwardly in the straw.

"It's all right, Midnight. I'm here," she breathed. "How are you feeling today?" At the sound of Ashleigh's voice, Midnight nickered again and tried to struggle to his feet. His forelegs thrashed around as he attempted to use his good hind leg to prop himself up. With a resigned snort, he sank back down and let out another nicker of pain, only to begin struggling once more. Ashleigh winced. A racehorse's hind legs provided most of his power. It was horrible to see how useless Midnight's leg was to him now.

Ashleigh couldn't bear to see the expression in Midnight's eyes—he was frustrated and in pain, and couldn't understand why. She rushed into his stall and buried her head in his mane.

"I know you don't understand what's happening, Midnight. I wish I could explain it to you." She stroked his velvety black muzzle, trying to comfort him.

"How is he?" Jonas's gruff voice came over the stall door.

"He's been trying to get up," Ashleigh said. "I wish I could help him."

"He's a tough cookie, that one," Jonas replied. "He's not going to ask for help from anyone. He wants to do it himself."

Midnight seemed to respond to Jonas's words. Ashleigh jumped back as he heaved himself to his feet with a mighty effort. Shaking his mane, he let out a loud, victorious whinny. Ashleigh laughed. If Midnight wanted to help himself, that was half the battle won.

"He's got spirit," Jonas said. "You have to give him that."

"He sure has," Ashleigh said fondly, tickling Midnight behind his ears. He had such a sweet personality. The pain might have driven another horse to behave viciously, but not Midnight.

Midnight's ears flicked back and forth at the sound of footfalls in the aisle, and a moment later Ashleigh's parents appeared at the stall door.

"He got up all by himself," Ashleigh told them, not mentioning the effort it had taken him, or the pain she'd seen in Midnight's eyes.

"Well, it's a good start," Mr. Griffen said gravely. "But don't go expecting miracles from him, Ashleigh. You heard what Dr. Frankel said. There's a risk of infection, and he's going to be in a lot of pain over the next few days."

"I know, I know," Ashleigh said. "But I'm going to stay with him all the time." She tried to ignore the worried look on her parents' faces. "First I'm going to groom him so well that he'll feel a hundred times better."

"Well, that's good, but go easy on him," her father said. "He'll need time on his own to come to terms with that cast."

Ashleigh nodded, but she had no intention of leaving Midnight alone. She had to help him get better. He could hurt himself thrashing around in his stall. If she was with him, he would stay calm.

Jonas and her father went off to talk over plans for the week ahead, leaving her mother behind.

"We'll all be here to help, too," Mrs. Griffen said. "You don't have to do it all on your own. Two weeks is a long time. We can take turns checking on him, poor thing. We've just got to hope that the leg starts to heal."

Pain gripped Ashleigh's heart when she saw her mother looking at Midnight's cast. *I didn't stop the fight,* she thought guiltily. She had actually urged Midnight on! Now Midnight's leg was broken. If only her mother knew . . . but Ashleigh couldn't bring herself to explain that it was all her fault.

"We've got to deal with this tragedy as best we can," Mrs. Griffen went on. "We have to carry on as normally as possible."

"I know, I know," Ashleigh said with a sigh. "But I'm going to do everything I can to help him." She picked up a body brush and began to brush Midnight's black coat.

"That's it," Mrs. Griffen encouraged. "Look, I've got to go and help your father, but I'll be back in a minute."

"Okay." Ashleigh nodded. She worked the body brush over Midnight's coat in smooth motions. The

44

black yearling looked tired. He hardly seemed to know what was going on.

"You'll be back to your old self soon," Ashleigh said softly. "I promise." She had to keep saying these things—for her own sake as much as Midnight's.

"Ashleigh, when you've finished in there, do you think you could help Jonas take the rest of the horses out to the paddocks?" Mrs. Griffen's head popped back over the stall door.

"But Mom—"

"No buts," Mrs. Griffen said firmly. "I know you want to be with him, but the farm still has to run as usual, no matter what's happened. And don't forget you've got Stardust to look after, too."

"Yes, all right," Ashleigh sighed. Closing the door to Midnight's stall, she hurried down the aisle. She couldn't even bear to look at Sparky as she passed his stall. She knew it wasn't really his fault that Midnight had broken his leg, but she couldn't help blaming him.

Stardust's head appeared over her stall door at the sound of Ashleigh's steps, and she whinnied happily when she saw Ashleigh approach. Slipping a halter over the mare's head, Ashleigh led her out to the paddocks.

"I haven't got time to ride you today," she said, stroking Stardust's neck as they walked through the paddock gate. "I hope you understand, but I need to spend time with Midnight. We'll go out together soon," Ashleigh promised, and stood back to let the mare off her lead shank. Then she went back into the barn to bring out Althea and Go Gen.

Once the horses were out in the paddocks, Ashleigh hurried back to Midnight's stall.

"He's fretting . . . been practically climbing the walls to get out," Jonas called across to her. Ashleigh grimaced as she watched Midnight lean his head over the stall door and swing it from side to side. In frustration he pawed at the floor, digging up the straw.

"I guess he doesn't like being cooped up in here when all the others are outside," she said.

"You can say that again," Jonas agreed. "He might be hurt, but his mind's all there. He wants to be outside in the fresh air, eating grass. He's so young—it's going to be hard for him when he discovers he can't do all the things he used to do."

"Well, I guess this first day's going to be the worst," Ashleigh said, stroking Midnight's nose.

"I'll keep an eye on him if you and Mona want to go out riding," Jonas offered.

Mona! Ashleigh suddenly remembered. Her friend had no idea what had happened. Ashleigh wasn't looking forward to reliving the accident, but Mona wouldn't want to be left in the dark.

"Jonas, do you think you could just stay with him for

five minutes? I've got to call Mona and tell her what happened."

"Sure thing," Jonas answered.

With a heavy step, Ashleigh made her way back into the house. Caroline was up and about in the kitchen when she walked in. "Just in time for breakfast," she said.

"I don't want anything," Ashleigh answered, already halfway down the hallway and heading for the phone.

Quickly she dialed Mona's number. Ashleigh bit her lip, fighting back the tears as she heard her friend's voice. Slowly Ashleigh told Mona about the accident, what the vet had said, and what her parents had decided to do. "I didn't tell my parents that I saw it and Caroline covered for me, but it *was* my fault," Ashleigh explained. "So I'm going to stay with him every minute of the day, until he gets better," she finished.

"Ashleigh, I'm sure it wasn't your fault. It was just an accident," Mona reassured her.

"I was *there*," Ashleigh insisted. "I could have stopped them if I'd tried." She took a deep breath. "Anyway, the vet said that if we keep him quiet, there's a chance the bone will start to heal. I'm not going to be able to skip school, but . . ."

Mona was silent.

"Mona, are you still there?"

"Yeah, I'm still here, Ash." Mona sighed. "It doesn't

sound good, though, does it? I just can't stand the thought of that sweet horse in so much pain."

"I know," Ashleigh said, suppressing a sob.

"Sometimes it's better to just let the horse go painlessly, you know," Mona said quietly.

"What do you mean?" Ashleigh cried out in disbelief. "We can't just put him down without giving him a chance!"

"Don't be angry with me," Mona said. "I'm just trying to be realistic."

Ashleigh blew out her breath in frustration. Why didn't everyone see how important it was to do everything possible to get Midnight better? "Look, I'll see you on the bus tomorrow, okay? Right now Midnight needs me."

Ashleigh felt bad as she hung up the phone. Mona was only trying to be sensible, but she had said the very words that Ashleigh didn't want to hear. Ashleigh couldn't even think about the possibility of putting Midnight down.

In a daze Ashleigh made her way to the barn. Her heart felt heavy as she walked down the aisle. Jonas was still with Midnight. Rory was at his side, anxiously looking at the black colt standing dejectedly in the straw.

"Sorry, I was a little longer than I thought," Ashleigh said. "But I can take over now."

Jonas nodded. "I had to give him another shot of ace, so he'll probably be pretty quiet. I'm going to help your parents with the yearlings. Give me a yell if you need anything."

"Thanks, Jonas," Ashleigh said.

"Can I help, Ash?" Rory pleaded.

Ashleigh hesitated. Rory loved Midnight as much as she did. It would be wrong to say no. "Well, there's not a lot we can do," Ashleigh explained. "But if you want to stay with him, too, why don't you go get a book to read with me in here?" she suggested.

"Okay, Ash." Rory paused and glanced first at the colt, then at Ashleigh. "He looks really sad, doesn't he? Not like he used to be."

"He's just sleepy from the painkillers, Rory," Ashleigh told him. "But he's going to have to take them for a while, so we have to get used to him acting different."

Rory looked upset. After a moment he said in a small voice, "Remember when he was little, and he used to get out of his stall and walk around the lawn eating Mom's flowers?"

"Yeah," Ashleigh said with a laugh. "He was so sneaky, wasn't he? Mom and Dad had to change the bolt on his stall so that he couldn't open it."

Rory smiled, and Ashleigh felt a little better.

"Look, Rory, as soon as Midnight's better, he'll be doing those funny things again," Ashleigh said. "Now go and get your book so you can read to us."

"All right." Rory disappeared off toward the house as Ashleigh slipped into Midnight's stall. Talking to Rory had brought back such precious memories—memories that turned painful as Ashleigh looked at the injured colt. Midnight turned away listlessly when she tried to pet him. Ashleigh felt her chest tighten, and she forced herself to think positive thoughts. *He's going to be all right. He just has to be.* She winced as she saw the yearling struggling to move his bad leg a little. He turned his head, trying to bite at the cast, but he couldn't reach.

"Oh, Midnight," Ashleigh cried, and hugged the colt's sleek black neck. "The cast is going to help you, honest it is. You've got to keep still. Promise me you won't do anything silly."

Midnight pawed at the ground, and Ashleigh grimaced.

"No, don't do that," she said. "Take it easy."

The colt seemed to settle down, and Ashleigh leaned against the side of the stall. A moment later Caroline's voice came from the aisle. "Ash? I brought you something." Ashleigh glanced up to see her sister holding out Prince Charming, her kitten. "I thought he might miss you if you're going to be in here all day."

"Hey, thanks," Ashleigh said, taking the kitten in her arms. Caroline was being so nice—it was a welcome change from the fights they sometimes got into.

"How is he?" Caroline asked, nodding in Midnight's direction.

"Sort of cranky and restless," Ashleigh reported. "But I think he's settling down."

Caroline nodded.

"I'm just worried about what's going to happen to him when we're at school tomorrow." Ashleigh turned back and patted Midnight's neck. "Mom and Dad and Jonas are going to be busy with the other horses, and Midnight needs to have someone with him."

"I don't know," Caroline said. "I heard Mom and Dad saying he'd need time to adjust to the injury. It might be good to leave him alone for a while."

Ashleigh swallowed hard. "Yeah, Dad said something like that to me, too." But the last thing she wanted was to leave Midnight alone.

As Caroline turned to leave, Ashleigh sat down in the straw with Prince Charming on her lap.

"Midnight's going to be all right, isn't he, Prince?" she asked, stroking the kitten and looking up at Midnight. But Ashleigh's words sounded hollow, even to her own ears. She remembered the look on Dr. Frankel's face the day before—he hadn't seemed very hopeful. Midnight was severely injured, and as much as Ashleigh hated to admit it, it was going to take a near miracle to get him well again.

4

Ashleigh had a difficult time leaving Midnight the next morning. As she stood at the end of the drive, waiting for her bus, all she wanted to do was turn around and run back to the barn.

When she climbed onto the school bus and saw Mona sitting in their usual spot, she felt a little embarrassed, remembering how she'd practically hung up on her friend the day before. But Mona seemed to have forgotten the matter, and she gave Ashleigh a sympathetic hug.

"How is everything, Ash?"

Ashleigh shrugged and looked out of the window, a lump rising in her throat. "Oh, you know. We've just got to wait and see. Only time will tell," she said, repeating all the expressions she'd heard over and over again that weekend. "He's a lot calmer anyway, and . . ." But all of a sudden Ashleigh couldn't hold the truth back any longer. "It's awful! He's in real pain, Mona," she burst out. "I can't be with him all the time. If he doesn't keep quiet, the break will never start to heal. And if he's not better in two weeks, the vet might have to—" The rest of Ashleigh's words turned into a muffled sob as she buried her head in Mona's shoulder. "I'm sorry I was so mean on the phone yesterday."

"Come on. Don't worry." Mona offered her friend a tissue. "It'll be all right. Your parents know what they're doing."

Ashleigh blew her nose, pulling herself together. "I'm sorry to be such a crybaby."

"Don't be sorry," Mona said. "It's good to let it all out. You sounded so funny on the phone yesterday that I had a feeling you were just storing it all up. Now come on. I bet you forgot we're getting that impossible math test back today," she said with a smile.

"Oh, great," Ashleigh groaned. She touched her friend's elbow. "Mona," she said, "please don't tell everyone at school what happened. I don't really feel like explaining everything."

"All right," Mona reassured her, "I won't."

"Ashleigh . . ." Mr. Gates, the fifth-grade math teacher, circled the class with the corrected test papers in his hand. He put hers on her desk and moved on. "Corey . . ."

Ashleigh didn't particularly want to turn the math test over, but she had to look at the grade sooner or later. She crossed her fingers. Maybe it wouldn't be as bad as she thought. She lifted up the corner of the paper, and a big red mark glared out at her—D minus. It was worse than she'd thought. Her grade had gone down three notches from the last test. Her parents would be furious.

"How did you do?" Mona whispered over from her desk.

"Don't ask," Ashleigh answered, already seeing the sorry scene with her parents flash before her eyes. "D minus . . . what did you get?"

"B plus," Mona said in an apologetic voice.

Mona was a whiz at math and always tried to help Ashleigh with her homework, so Ashleigh knew she wasn't gloating.

Ashleigh was so wrapped up in her thoughts, she could hardly keep her eyes on the board as Mr. Gates started to go over the test. Why couldn't she find math simple, like Mona or Caro? *Maybe it's because I don't pay enough attention in class,* Ashleigh thought. Still, what use was math going to be when all she wanted to do when she grew up was to be a jockey? Ashleigh stared out of the window at the football field. She imagined herself far from the stuffy classroom, riding Wanderer's Quest down to the start of the Preakness at Pimlico. The wind rustled her racing silks as she loaded into the starting gate. The barriers went down and they were off, racing down the track. Ashleigh settled herself in the middle of the pack as the horses jostled for position.

They were speeding along with just four horses ahead of them when they came around the last corner and into the top of the homestretch. Quest was getting faster and faster, wearing down each of her rivals. A gap appeared, and Ashleigh pushed Quest through to challenge the lead. Now she was racing down the inside rail and—

"Ashleigh! Are you listening to me?" Ashleigh was brought back to reality by the sound of Mr. Gates's voice.

"Yes . . . yes, I'm listening," Ashleigh faltered.

"Then perhaps you'd like to tell me how to solve this problem."

Ashleigh looked at the problem the teacher was indicating on the board, and her stomach sank. It was one of the ones she'd gotten wrong.

Just at that moment the bell sounded and everyone started packing up their bags. Ashleigh breathed a sigh of relief.

"Don't forget to leave your homework on my desk as you leave," Mr. Gates called above the din.

Ashleigh deposited her pages of scribbled problems on the pile and filed out of the room. It was lunchtime, and Ashleigh felt a rumble of hunger as she and Mona made their way to the cafeteria.

"I'll help you study next time," Mona reassured her.

"Thanks," Ashleigh said. "I'm going to have to work pretty hard when my parents hear about this grade."

"Well, what if I come by your house tomorrow?" Mona suggested. "We could go over some problems, and if I bring Frisky, we could take a quick trail ride afterward."

"Okay." Ashleigh tried to sound enthusiastic, although riding was the last thing on her mind. She wanted to spend all her free time with Midnight.

"Great!" Mona grinned. "And don't worry—we'll get your math grade back up."

"Thanks," Ashleigh said, attempting a smile.

"Ashleigh! Mona!" Ashleigh turned to see her friend Lynne Duran running toward her. Lynne was as crazy about horses as Ashleigh and Mona were. She'd spent the weekend at Gulfstream Park in Florida and was bursting to tell Mona and Ashleigh all about it.

As they got in line for food, Jamie Wilson, another riding friend, joined them. Mona was as good as her word and didn't mention Midnight's accident.

"Are you sure you want to hear a complete replay of everything that happened at Gulfstream?" Lynne asked with a chuckle.

"Of course we do." Ashleigh grinned, doing her best

to be cheerful. "Hearing about it is almost as good as being there."

"I can't wait till racing starts closer to home," Jamie said.

Ashleigh nodded. Tickets to the races were expensive, but her parents sometimes managed to take her to one of the Kentucky tracks—Keeneland or Turfway Park. Churchill Downs was Ashleigh's favorite.

Ashleigh picked out a grilled cheese sandwich and fries, then paid and made her way to their usual table.

"So tell us already, Lynne," Ashleigh said as they sat down.

"Well." Lynne took a deep breath. "There were eleven races in all. The day went so quickly. Supreme Sound was running, and I haven't seen him run live since he won the Breeders' Cup. Of course Dad wasn't around much, since he had to call the races, so I had to entertain myself, but I didn't mind that. I just wandered around the backside. I got to see every race. It was so cool. There were four photo finishes—can you believe it?"

"Wow!" Ashleigh exclaimed. "I'm jealous."

"Well, you shouldn't be." Lynne laughed. "You have all those cute foals to play with all the time."

Ashleigh thought of Midnight and swallowed uneasily. *But she's right,* Ashleigh reminded herself. Jamie and Lynne lived in town, so their horses had to be boarded at local riding stables. Nothing could compare to waking up to see horses on your own land.

"So how's Stardust going?" Jamie asked through a mouthful of her sandwich.

"Oh, you know, the usual," Ashleigh answered, feeling even more depressed as she was reminded of the mare. She hadn't paid any attention to Stardust since Midnight's accident.

"Is something wrong?" Lynne asked.

"It's—it's nothing important," Ashleigh said, pushing away her plate of food, suddenly not feeling very hungry. Mona looked at her sympathetically.

Lynne and Jamie looked at Ashleigh, then at Mona, then at each other, but they didn't pursue the matter. "So how are the yearlings?" Lynne asked.

Oh, no, Ashleigh thought. "Just fine," she said, her voice wavering, her eyes beginning to fill with tears.

"Have any of them been sold yet?" Jamie asked.

"No, not yet." Ashleigh grimaced. "Sorry, guys, I've got to go change for gym," she announced, standing up. "Mona," she whispered, nudging her friend, "you'd better tell them."

"I'll save you a spot on the bus," Mona called as Ashleigh left.

When the bell sounded at the end of the school day, Ashleigh was out of the door like a shot. Not since she'd first gotten Stardust had she been so anxious to leave school. Mona had told their friends about the accident, and when they'd seen each other in the hallway later they'd all rallied around Ashleigh, but seeing their sympathetic faces had almost made things worse for her.

The bus dropped Ashleigh off at Edgardale at three-thirty. She had five and a half hours ahead of her to spend with Midnight before she'd have to go to bed. But as Ashleigh hurried up the drive to the barn, the sound of hysterical neighing filled the air. Her heart pounded. *Midnight!* She broke into a run and dashed into the barn. It took a moment for her eyes to adjust to the dim interior as she raced to the end stall.

The sight that greeted her filled her with horror. Midnight was lying down, his front legs scrambling frantically as he tried to stand. His eyes were rolling as he lashed out, turning to bite at his cast and scraping at the floor with his hooves.

"Midnight, Midnight . . . easy, don't do that," Ashleigh breathed.

At the sound of Ashleigh's voice, Midnight checked himself, but Ashleigh could see he was in a lot of pain. Thrashing around in his stall had probably made his leg hurt even more. *The bute must have worn off,* Ashleigh thought. *He needs another shot.*

Ashleigh bit her bottom lip. Though she'd seen her parents and Jonas do it dozens of times, she'd never given a horse a shot before. Her parents wouldn't like it, but this was different. It would take too long to go looking for them.

"I'll be back in just a minute, boy. Stay calm," Ashleigh called, unable to keep the terror out of her voice.

She sprinted to the barn office, where her parents kept the horse medication. Anxiously Ashleigh pulled out the drawers, each neatly labeled with the name of a different medication. *This is hopeless,* she thought. *Where did they put the bute?* Then she turned to the desk and saw a package. She turned it over. Phenylbutazone—that was it. Her parents hadn't put it away. Ashleigh grabbed a plastic-wrapped syringe and made her way back to Midnight's stall. The sounds were getting louder and louder now, and Ashleigh felt her hands start to tremble. She opened the stall door and fumbled with the shot. *In his neck, that's where it has to go. Just like I've seen it done so many times.*

"Easy does it." She took a deep breath and got ready to stick the needle in.

"Ashleigh, is that you? Are you back already?" The sound of her father's voice floated down the aisle, and Ashleigh felt a wave of relief flood through her.

"In here," she called, hiding the syringe behind her back.

"How's he doing?" Mr. Griffen looked over the stall door.

"I think he needs another shot," Ashleigh said, trying to keep her voice from trembling. "Here," she said, thrusting the syringe into her father's hand.

"Ashleigh!" Mr. Griffen exclaimed, looking surprised.

"Please, Dad," Ashleigh said. "Look at him."

Midnight was still lying down. He lifted his head and grunted as he tried to prop his good hind leg underneath him once more. But he stopped there, as if he just couldn't make the effort to try to stand. He looked miserable.

"All right," her father said, going into the stall. "Maybe you're right. He hasn't had any bute since lunchtime." He unwrapped the syringe. "Easy, boy," he said. Crouching down, he plunged the needle into Midnight's neck.

Midnight didn't flinch, and as the bute began to work, Ashleigh could see the tense colt relax.

"You know, loading him up with painkillers isn't going to do anything to heal his leg," he father reminded her. "All it does is keep him comfortable."

"I know," Ashleigh admitted.

"It will help him get used to the cast, though," Mr. Griffen said. He patted Ashleigh's shoulder. "Don't worry," he added. "There's still time."

Ashleigh nodded, but she couldn't help feeling more worried than ever.

After finishing her chores, Ashleigh sat with Midnight, doing her homework in his stall. Midnight was standing now, pulling hay from his hay net, and Ashleigh was mulling over an English comprehension question when Jonas came by and leaned on the stall door.

"Ashleigh, Stardust missed you today."

Ashleigh looked up. "I know. I just can't leave Midnight," she explained. "He's so sad—you can tell his leg is hurting."

"He's a pretty brave guy." Jonas nodded in Midnight's direction, looking him up and down. "And he looks quiet now. I don't want to get your hopes up," Jonas continued, "but if we can get him to stay quiet like that all the time, he might have a chance."

Ashleigh sucked in her breath. It was the first bit of positive thinking she'd heard since the accident, and if Jonas was right, she would have to find a way to stay with Midnight all the time. She had to keep him quiet.

Jonas shrugged. "It's a bad injury, I'm not denying that, but it's not impossible. When I was working up in New York we had a racehorse there who fractured her cannon bone, just like Midnight. She was called Golden Fleece—a beautiful bay mare. It broke my heart see her in such pain."

"But she got better?" Ashleigh demanded excitedly.

"Oh, she got better, all right," Jonas said. "She was a four-year-old, so she was a lot more worldly-wise than Midnight here, and a lot more patient, too. Nobody thought she would recover, but she did. She never raced again, and it was pretty hard for her owners, but at least they were able to breed her. She produced twelve healthy foals and lived till she was twenty-five."

Ashleigh felt a little better. But Midnight was only a yearling, and unraced at that. He was completely different from a proven race winner. What would they do with him when this was all over? She didn't dare think such thoughts.

The black colt chewed slowly on his hay, his neck shining beneath the barn light. He was still beautiful, still magnificent. The cast was the only sign that anything was wrong with him. Ashleigh looked at her watch. It was dinnertime, and she ought to be getting inside.

"Thanks, Jonas," she said, smiling as she grabbed her jacket from the hook by Midnight's stall. "See you tomorrow."

"Night, Ashleigh," Jonas said.

As she walked down the aisle, she felt a ray of hope flood through her. Maybe Midnight would be all right. She ran across the grass, pulled back the screen door, and walked into the kitchen. Her mother and father were sitting at the kitchen table, engrossed in a pile of paperwork.

"Dinner's almost ready," her mother said, looking up. Her father began to shuffle the papers into a pile.

"Mom, Dad . . . is everything all right?" Ashleigh said.

"Just fine," Mr. Griffen said calmly. Ashleigh thought he still looked worried, but she didn't want to press him.

Mrs. Griffen stood up and went into the hallway. "Rory, Caroline. Dinner," she called.

Ashleigh sat down next to her father. "I was just talking to Jonas," she said breathlessly. "He said that if we keep Midnight really quiet, he really could get better. And he told me about this mare up in New York. She broke her cannon bone like Midnight—but it healed just fine," she added.

Mr. Griffen sighed. "Jonas was trying to make you feel better, but he knows—and he should have told you—that a good outcome like that is not common." Then, seeing the hurt look on Ashleigh's face, he softened. "I'm sorry, Ashleigh. I know you want Midnight to get well. We all do. But I think you need to know the truth."

Ashleigh looked at her father, unable to speak for a moment. Jonas had given her reason to hope, and her father had completely crushed it.

"Dad," she started slowly, "I was wondering . . . I mean, would it be all right if I stayed with Midnight tonight? He's lonely and he needs company. I didn't ask you before because I knew you had enough on your mind. But he's so much calmer when I'm around."

"Ashleigh . . ." Mr. Griffen looked wearily at his daughter.

"Just for tonight," Ashleigh said. "Please? He needs to know I'm there for him."

"I don't know," her father argued. "It's a school night. I'll have to talk to your mother about it."

"But if you say yes, I'm sure she will, too," Ashleigh wheedled.

Mr. Griffen rolled his eyes. "All right, then—I suppose one night won't hurt."

"What won't hurt?" Mrs. Griffen asked as she came back into the kitchen.

"I just told Ashleigh she could stay in the barn with Midnight tonight," Mr. Griffen explained.

Mrs. Griffen looked at her husband wordlessly for a moment. Then she let out a sigh, and when her gaze met Ashleigh's her eyes were full of sympathy. "All right, Ashleigh. You'd probably sneak out there anyway. But first we're having dinner."

"You're nuts, Ash . . . do you know that?" Caroline heaved a pile of blankets into Midnight's stall and dropped them onto the straw.

Midnight flinched.

"Hey, watch out!" Ashleigh said.

"Sorry." Caroline looked sheepish as Ashleigh knelt down beside Midnight and patted his neck.

Midnight was lying down, bundled into a warm New Zealand rug, with his forelegs curled beneath him. He watched curiously as Ashleigh settled in beside him for the night.

She had plenty of blankets, and the straw made a soft bed, but it was cold and dark in the barn, and Ashleigh was starting to feel a little nervous about staying out there on her own all night.

"There you are." Mrs. Griffen came up behind Caroline and positioned the portable electric heater outside the stall. "Now, have you got enough clothes on?"

"I think so." Ashleigh raised her arms. "A T-shirt and two sweatshirts, leggings and jeans, and two pairs of wool socks. If all this doesn't keep me warm, nothing will."

"Wait, I brought you something, Ash." Rory poked his head around the stall door. His face looked mournful as he pulled Prince Charming out of his coat. "I wanted to stay out with Midnight, too, but Mom and Dad said I couldn't." He handed over the kitten. "Prince Charming can stay with you guys instead."

"Thanks, Rory," Ashleigh said, smiling as she tucked the kitten into the pile of blankets. Prince Charming and Midnight blinked at each other, and Ashleigh laughed. "Midnight's not going to be lonely tonight."

"He should be all right during the night," Mrs. Griffen said. "I gave him a shot of bute at feeding time. But promise us that you'll go get Jonas or call us from the barn phone if there's a problem."

"Okay. And could you leave the tack room light on for me?" Ashleigh said. Her mother nodded, and Ashleigh's family made their way back to the house.

Ashleigh settled down beside Midnight, pulling the blanket up over her shoulder and tucking Prince Charming beneath her arm. Midnight was quiet as he lay in the straw, his breath coming slow and steady as he closed his eyes in sleep. It was sad to see him looking so lifeless. He hadn't been his old self in days.

Ashleigh didn't think she'd ever get to sleep, but the long day was beginning to catch up with her, and finally she nestled down in her blankets and slept.

It wasn't until the next morning that Ashleigh woke up. At first she couldn't remember where she was. Then, when she felt the straw underneath her and breathed in the soft horse smells she loved so much, she remembered.

But her body was stiff and her head felt like lead. At first she thought it was from sleeping on the stall floor, but then she sneezed, and she realized she'd developed a cold during the night. *Good, maybe I can stay home from school today,* she thought.

Midnight was still asleep next to her, and Ashleigh didn't want to wake him. She shivered as she pulled the blanket up over her. Prince Charming rolled over and curled up again. Then Midnight stretched out his neck and let out a big-toothed yawn. Ashleigh sat up as the yearling heaved himself up onto his feet and shook himself. Midnight tried to take a step toward Ashleigh, sniffing the blankets, but when he tried to put weight on his bad hind leg, his head shot up. Ashleigh could see he was in pain. She wanted so badly to help him, but what could she do?

"It's all right, boy," Ashleigh called groggily.

She dragged herself to her feet and rubbed the yearling's black neck. He pinned his ears, shaking his head impatiently and rolling his eyes. Ashleigh released her hand in shock. Midnight had never behaved like this. The pain in his leg must be driving him crazy.

Ashleigh hurried out of the stall and made her way to the barn office. It was dark in the aisle; even Jonas wasn't up and about yet. Ashleigh didn't want to wake him—she'd just have to give Midnight the bute herself this time.

Ashleigh rubbed her eyes sleepily as she went over to the cabinet where they kept the medication. She opened up the drawer with Midnight's name on it and fumbled around inside until she found the brute. Then she made her way back to his stall.

Midnight was weaving his head back and forth. He didn't even glance at Ashleigh as she opened his stall door.

"It's okay, Midnight. It's all right, boy," Ashleigh crooned. She held her breath as she stuck the needle into the yearling's neck, just as she'd seen her father do.

Midnight didn't even protest. Gently she withdrew the needle, recapped it, and stuffed the syringe in her jacket pocket. She stroked Midnight's neck to comfort him, but the yearling just hung his head over the stall door.

Ashleigh frowned and looked out the barn door. The sky above the paddocks was beginning to lighten, and already she could hear the horses moving around in their stalls. Just another day at Edgardale, and yet things weren't the same anymore and never would be again. She patted Midnight's neck.

"Now, I'm going to have to leave you alone for a while—just till I get my chores done," she whispered, leaving the stall and heading for the feed room.

Marvy Mary, Jolita, My Georgina, Stardust . . . Ashleigh made her way down the aisle, measuring out the food for each horse. As she reached Stardust's stall the mare lifted her head over her door and nickered excitedly. Ashleigh stroked her nose.

"Maybe after school we can go for a ride. You'd like that, huh?" Ashleigh said to the chestnut mare. "Mona and Frisky might come, too."

"How was Midnight during the night?" Ashleigh's thoughts were disturbed by her mother's voice.

"Okay, but he's been kind of restless this morning," Ashleigh replied hesitantly.

"The painkillers have worn off by now. I'd better give him a shot," Mrs. Griffen said, heading for the office.

"Yes, well, um . . ." Ashleigh searched for the right words. She didn't want to tell her mother she'd given Midnight a shot without permission, but it could do more harm than good for Midnight to have another shot right away. Ashleigh would have to confess.

"Mom, I already gave him one," she admitted.

"You did?" Mrs. Griffen looked surprised. "I asked you to get Jonas or us if there was a problem with Midnight during the night."

"Well, I've see everyone do it so many times, and so I just copied you," Ashleigh said defensively.

"You're too young to give horses medication. It could be very dangerous if something went wrong," Mrs. Griffen reprimanded her. "I don't want you ever doing that again. Do you understand?"

"All right," Ashleigh sniffed, feeling ashamed.

"I know you have your heart set on getting Midnight better, so I won't say anything more this time." Mrs.

Griffen raised her eyebrows. "Caroline and Rory will be down in a minute. Finish your stalls, then go up to the house and take a hot shower. I'm going to make you some oatmeal."

Ashleigh had thought about asking to stay home from school that day, using her cold as an excuse to sit with Midnight. But her mother had been so understanding about Midnight's shot that Ashleigh didn't want to push her luck. She would just have to pull herself together and get on that school bus.

5

Ashleigh's cold was getting worse and worse. As she made her way up the drive after school that afternoon, she felt light-headed and sleepy. She hated to admit it, but staying out in the barn on a cold winter's night hadn't been such a great idea after all. Her nose was streaming and her head was throbbing. She didn't know how she'd managed to get through a whole day of classes, but she certainly hadn't been concentrating very hard.

She let out a loud sneeze as she climbed the stairs to the house.

"Is that you, Ash?" Her mother hurried into the kitchen. "I'm so glad you're here. I just got off the phone with Mr. Danworth. Do you remember him?"

"Mr. Danworth? The man who bought Aladdin?" Ashleigh's head might be foggy, but she never forgot an owner. Mr. Danworth had bought a beautiful black colt from them the year before last for his training farm in Florida.

"That's right," Mrs. Griffen answered with a smile. "Well, he just called. He wants to come up on Saturday and take a look at our yearlings."

Ashleigh immediately understood why her mother looked so pleased. Mr. Danworth had paid $80,000 for Aladdin—the most they'd ever gotten for a yearling up until then.

"Great, Mom," Ashleigh said, trying to sound enthusiastic. But her voice sounded stuffed-up and hoarse.

"Oh, Ashleigh, you're getting a cold." Mrs. Griffen felt Ashleigh's forehead. "We shouldn't have let you stay out in the barn last night."

"I'll be okay, Mom," Ashleigh said, although she was starting to feel a little wobbly.

"You're going straight to bed to rest," Mrs. Griffen said, steering Ashleigh toward the stairs.

"But I've got to go to the barn. I haven't been out to see Midnight yet, and I haven't ridden Stardust in days. I said I'd take her out after school, and Mona is supposed to be coming over."

"Stardust can wait another couple of days till you're better," Mrs. Griffen said firmly, gently pushing Ashleigh in the direction of the stairs. "I'll call Mona, and Jonas will look after Midnight. He'll be all right without you for one day. You're not going to do anyone any good as sick as you are."

*   *   *

Ashleigh's cold turned rapidly to flu. Her head grew hot with fever, and she wound up in bed for the rest of the week. Every waking moment she thought of Midnight, but the next thing she knew, Caroline would be shaking her awake with a cup of tea, explaining that she'd been asleep again for hours. Finally on Saturday her fever broke and she felt much better.

That afternoon Ashleigh sat on the sofa, curled up under her comforter. She took a sip out of the steaming mug of soup that her mother had left with her, and picked up a horse magazine. She tried to read, but the words swam before her eyes. There was no one to talk to, either. Her parents were out in the barn getting the yearlings ready for Mr. Danworth, Caroline had gone into town shopping with friends, Rory was outside playing, and Ashleigh had already phoned Mona to tell her that she wasn't up to going riding yet. The house was quiet, and Ashleigh was seriously bored.

She picked up the remote control and flicked through the channels. There was nothing good on TV—it would be a whole two hours till the afternoon's horse racing coverage started.

Ashleigh's mind strayed to Midnight. A week had gone by since his accident. Only one week left before the vet came again.

Ashleigh got to her feet and looked out the window. She could see her father and Jonas in the paddocks, leading the yearlings out in their leather show halters.

Jonas was leading the dappled gray filly, Rosie, who kicked up her heels and skipped around at the end of her lead line. Her father led Sparky, who was behaving himself for once. Ashleigh shivered as she watched the caramel-colored colt. It was hard to look at him without thinking about the accident.

Ashleigh pushed the thought to the back of her mind. All the yearlings were fantastic, and she would keep her fingers crossed that Mr. Danworth would want to buy one of them.

Moving away from the window, Ashleigh flopped back down on the sofa and picked up the horse magazine again as she sipped her soup. She looked briefly at the pictures before throwing it down on the floor. What did any of it matter when Midnight was alone in his stall?

Ashleigh felt restless. She couldn't stand just sitting there, not knowing what Midnight was up to or how he was feeling. Her mother had ordered her to stay in the house, but five minutes in the barn couldn't hurt.

Ashleigh wandered into the kitchen and put her soup mug in the sink. Through the window, she saw a sleek silver BMW drive up and park outside. She recognized the tall, smartly dressed man who got out as Mr. Danworth. Her mother walked over to greet him.

Ashleigh's mind raced. She could sneak out to the

barn to see Midnight while her parents were busy in the paddocks. They wouldn't even notice.

Ashleigh didn't stop to think twice. She grabbed a sweatshirt and headed for the door. Furtively she glanced into the paddocks as she crept across the gravel drive, but everyone was busy and she got to the barn without being seen.

It was quiet inside, with all of the horses out in the paddocks. Ashleigh made her way straight up the aisle to Midnight's stall. When he heard her footfall, his head appeared over the door and he nickered happily. Ashleigh felt a warm glow flood through her, but it rapidly disappeared as Midnight's head began to weave back and forth.

"You shouldn't be doing that, Midnight. That's a bad habit," Ashleigh murmured. The poor horse was clearly bored, and Ashleigh's heart went out to him. Midnight hated being cooped up in his stall just as much as she hated sitting in the house.

Ashleigh thought hard. What Midnight really needed was a change of scene. What if she led him out a little way? Just over to the door of the barn, so he could see all the other yearlings in the paddocks. His was the end stall—it was only twenty feet from the door. Besides, he was used to walking on three legs now. She was sure he could make it.

"There's a good boy, there you are," Ashleigh said as

she clipped a lead shank to his halter and gave it a little tug.

Midnight seemed surprised at first, but then he began to follow her. With his attention fixed on the door to the outdoors, already the black horse looked happier—his ears were pricked and his eyes were animated. Although he was eager to get to the door, he could barely put any weight on the toe of his injured leg, and Ashleigh felt as though her heart might break as she watched him hobble along.

"Come on, Midnight. You can do it," Ashleigh encouraged him. "We're nearly there now." He let out a small, pitiful nicker. "Just another few steps, Midnight," she coaxed.

One step, two steps, three, and finally they were there. Midnight stood in the doorway of the barn and looked around him. He sniffed the air inquisitively, his ears flickering back and forth. Ashleigh watched him looking at the horses in the paddocks beyond the trees. She could see Jonas and her father leading the yearlings out while Mrs. Griffen stood talking to Mr. Danworth. Ashleigh patted Midnight's neck as he let out a huge whinny, calling to the other horses.

"Shhh! Mom and Dad aren't supposed to know you're out here," Ashleigh said, looking anxiously toward the paddocks. Nobody seemed to have noticed them, and she breathed a sigh of relief.

Just a few moments longer, Ashleigh thought, pleased to see how happy Midnight was to be out in the open.

The yearling tugged a little at the lead shank, getting more and more excited as he looked this way and that. His nostrils were flared, and Ashleigh knew he'd be off in a second if he could. Midnight whinnied a second time, and Sparky whirled around to see who was calling.

"We'd better get you back inside, Midnight," Ashleigh said nervously. Jonas was taking the halters off the yearlings. Her parents looked as though they were finished showing the horses to Mr. Danworth. Ashleigh tugged on the lead shank, but Midnight resisted, yanking his head up. She wasn't prepared for how stubborn he could be.

"You're going to get me in a lot of trouble," Ashleigh pleaded.

Helplessly she tried to make Midnight turn around as she heard the voices on the path down to the barn. But it was too late—the group came around the corner, and Ashleigh was caught red-handed.

"Ashleigh!" Her mother looked angry. "What are you doing? Why is Midnight out of his stall? You know he's not supposed to be putting any weight on that leg!"

"I felt so sorry for him. It's not very far, and he's not hurting," Ashleigh answered.

"That's not the point," Mr. Griffen told her. "That horse needs stall rest."

"But he looked so depressed. He was weaving," Ashleigh spluttered. "I thought a change of scene might make him feel better. He hasn't walked far. . . ."

"Take him back into the barn, and then I want you back inside yourself," Mrs. Griffen said furiously. "We'll deal with this later."

"Wait a minute." Mr. Danworth stepped forward. "Which colt is this?"

"Well, he's registered under the name Midnight Wanderer." Mr. Griffen took a deep breath. "I didn't show him to you for obvious reasons."

"Yes, I see," Mr. Danworth said, looking Midnight up and down. "Very impressive conformation. Is he any relation to Wanderer's Quest?"

"Half-brother," Mr. Griffen said, walking over to stroke the colt's neck. "Same mother, and one of his grandsires was Affirmed, so he's got royal breeding."

"All of your horses seem to have good bloodlines." Mr. Danworth nodded at Midnight's cast. "What's wrong with his leg?"

"We were hoping for great things from this colt," Mr. Griffen said. "But he's fractured a cannon bone."

Ashleigh heard the devastation in her father's voice, though his face remained calm and matter-of-fact.

"He was playing around with one of the other yearlings in the paddock when it happened," Mrs. Griffen explained.

"A sad story—but a huge dent in your income, too, I'd think." Mr. Danworth raised his eyebrows. "So what are you keeping him on for? It's unlikely he'll ever race."

Ashleigh felt as if she'd been slapped in the face. Was money the only thing people could think of? Why didn't anyone seem to think it was important whether Midnight lived or not, even if he couldn't race?

"Oh, we know that," Mrs. Griffen said, glancing at Ashleigh. "Our vet said that if the fracture heals fairly well, he might make a decent pleasure horse. Considering his bloodlines, he could be used for stud, too."

"Hmm, maybe," Mr. Danworth said, but he didn't look altogether convinced.

Ashleigh had been trying to keep quiet, but what Mr. Danworth had said was the last thing she wanted her parents to hear. She just had to say something.

"Midnight's going to be fine," she burst out, her face red with anger. "Did you think we'd just put him down? We *care* about our horses here!"

The minute the words were out of her mouth, she regretted the way she'd said them. She hadn't meant to insult Mr. Danworth; she'd only wanted to protect Midnight.

"Ashleigh!" Mr. Griffen cried.

Mr. Danworth turned to look at Ashleigh. "You're young, Ashleigh. But as you get older you'll learn that caring means doing the best thing by your horse—and if he's in pain, then having him put down is sometimes the best way."

"Ashleigh didn't mean to be rude," Mrs. Griffen put in. "It's just that she's always taken care of Midnight, and his injury has been harder on her than any of us."

"I understand," Mr. Danworth said.

"Yes, I'm sorry I was rude," Ashleigh said, trying to make up for her outburst.

Midnight pawed at the ground. "Easy, boy," she said, tugging at the lead shank. "I guess I'd better put him back in his stall."

Ashleigh could feel Mr. Danworth watching as she turned Midnight around. She winced as the yearling hobbled into his stall after her.

"Shall we go over to the house and continue our talk about some of the other yearling prospects?" her father said.

Mr. Danworth was silent for a moment before he answered. "Well, actually, I think I'll give you a call later on this week. Now that I've seen this horse, I realize that your other yearlings may not be quite what I'm looking for. It's a shame this one is ruined now. With his conformation and those bloodlines, he might have been magnificent."

Ashleigh stayed in Midnight's stall. She wished they would go away. She didn't want to hear any more.

"I understand." Mr. Griffen's voice sounded reasonable, but Ashleigh heard the note of disappointment underneath the words. "Our other yearlings are very promising, though. I hope you'll consider them, too."

"Oh, Midnight, why can't I stop putting my foot in my mouth?" Ashleigh moaned softly to the colt as Mr. Danworth and her parents left the barn. "I'm always getting myself into trouble. Don't listen to what that man said. You're going to be all right, I'm sure of it."

She heard the BMW's motor as Mr. Danworth drove away. Midnight's accident had been all her fault, and now her parents had lost a sale because of her, too. She closed the door to Midnight's stall and left the barn to apologize.

With a sinking heart, she walked into the kitchen of the white farmhouse. It was empty. She padded down the hallway to her father's study and knocked on his door.

"Come in."

"It's only me, Dad." Ashleigh pushed back the door. "I just wanted to say how sorry I was for being rude to Mr. Danworth." She hung her head in shame.

Mr. Griffen looked at her and frowned. "What came over you, Ashleigh? Mr. Danworth didn't say anything unfair. Our clients are important to us. We can't go around insulting them."

"I know," Ashleigh said. "It's just that I thought I was doing the right thing taking Midnight out—he looked much happier. Then hearing Mr. Danworth talk about him like that made me realize how bad everything is. What if his leg doesn't heal?"

"We knew all of this when we decided to give Midnight a chance, Ash." Mr. Griffen patted her on the shoulder. "The vet will be back next week. Try not to worry."

Ashleigh nodded, feeling a lump rising in her throat as she closed the door and dragged herself upstairs to her bedroom. She sat down on her bed. She was supposed to be resting, but there was no way she could sleep. She wished she could talk to someone. Then she remembered her diary. Writing in it always made her feel better.

Ashleigh pulled her diary out from under her mattress and opened it up. She looked at the last entry she had made, when her parents had finally said Stardust could stay. Everything had seemed so promising then. She had ridden out on Stardust in a storm to find Rory and Moe, who'd gotten lost on the paths behind the farm, and the mare had gone so well for her, as though she'd known how important that ride was.

Stardust—it was the first time in days that Ashleigh had even thought about the copper-colored horse. Ashleigh sighed, pen poised, staring at the blank page. Finally she started writing, and the words came pouring out of her.

Dear Diary:

Do you remember Midnight Wanderer? The colt Rory called Tonka? Well, he got in a fight with Sparky and broke the cannon bone in his right hind leg. I saw the whole thing happen. I still think I should have stopped them, but I wanted Midnight to win. Caroline said it wasn't my fault, and she's being really nice about it.

Dr. Frankel said Midnight will never race, and he wanted to put him down. But we won't do that. I know Midnight's leg hurts a lot, but at least he's alive. Dr. Frankel put a cast on it, and he's coming back to look at him next week.

It's pretty sad at Edgardale right now. I wish something good would happen. Mom and Dad look worried all the time. I know they're worrying about money. Midnight was the most valuable yearling we had, and now everyone says he's not worth anything (although I know that's not true).

Mr. Danworth came today to look at the yearlings. He was going to buy one of them, but when he saw Midnight he changed his mind. If I hadn't let Midnight out of his stall, then Mr. Danworth would never have known about him. And as if that wasn't bad enough, I wasn't very nice to him.

I feel like everything is my fault. I don't know what I'll do if Midnight is put down.

Ashleigh turned to look out of the window at the paddocks below. This wasn't working. Writing everything down was making her feel worse, not better. She had to try to think positively.

As she sat there, a tear trickled down her cheek. Just then she heard the door downstairs slam shut and someone come running up the stairs. Ashleigh wiped her eyes with her sleeve and thrust the diary under her mattress just as Caroline flung open the door and marched in carrying two large shopping bags.

"Hi, Ash. How are you feeling?" Caroline asked breathlessly.

"Oh, a little better." Ashleigh smiled weakly.

"Well, come on." Caroline bounced down on her bed. "I want to show you all the goodies I bought."

"All right," Ashleigh agreed. She hated looking at clothes, but Caroline had been so nice to her lately that it was the least she could do.

"So, what do you think of this?" Caroline held up a pink minidress and modeled it against her.

"I guess it's nice," Ashleigh said, trying to sound enthusiastic.

"You can borrow it anytime you want," Caroline offered. "Come on, Ash, try it on," she added, spinning around the room.

Ashleigh was about to refuse—the only time she ever borrowed any of Caroline's clothes was when she couldn't find anything clean in one of the piles on the floor—but when she saw the look of disappointment on her sister's face, she gave in. "All right," she sighed. Quickly she struggled out of her jeans and into the outfit.

"Hey, Ash, you look great! And with these shoes . . ."

Ashleigh turned to look at herself in the mirror. The pink dress was big in all the wrong places and totally unflattering. She just didn't look like herself. "There, didn't I tell you you'd look good?" Caroline beamed. "Now just the hair . . ."

"No! No way!" Ashleigh cried.

They were interrupted by a knock at the door. Rory pushed it open and stumbled into the room.

"Mom says it's dinnertime, and—Ashleigh?" Rory burst into fits of giggles.

"What's so funny?" Ashleigh said, frowning at her reflection in the mirror.

"Nothing," Rory said, trying to suppress a giggle. "You look kind of weird, that's all. I mean, you in a pink dress!"

"That's it!" Ashleigh fumed. She pushed her little brother out the door.

"Ash, I didn't mean to make you mad." Rory's voice trailed off as Ashleigh slammed the door and wriggled out of the dress.

"Remind me never to listen to you again, Caroline," Ashleigh snapped.

"Oh, come on." Caroline tried to stifle her giggles. "Rory wasn't being mean—he's just not used to seeing you in anything besides jeans and a sweatshirt."

"Well, don't make me dress up in your stuff again," Ashleigh grouched.

"All right, all right," Caroline said, raising her hands in the air.

Ashleigh sat on her bed and looked at the pink dress lying in a heap on the floor. She picked it up and threw it at Caroline. She didn't like being laughed at, but she knew that Caroline was right. Rory hadn't meant any harm, and probably it *was* strange to see her in a dress.

Caroline sat down next to her and nudged Ashleigh with her elbow. Ashleigh let out a smile despite herself.

"You should have seen your face," Caroline giggled.

Then Ashleigh began to laugh, too, and soon the two girls were in stitches. Once she started, Ashleigh couldn't stop. Her laughter threw her into a fit of coughing, but still, it felt good. She hadn't laughed like that in days. Not since Midnight was hurt.

6

"Midnight," Ashleigh called on Monday afternoon. She hurried into the barn and made her way to Midnight's stall. The black horse nickered when he saw her, and Ashleigh felt pleased. He certainly looked bright and in good spirits. But Ashleigh knew the sad truth. Midnight was on so many painkillers that it was impossible to tell whether the injury was really getting better, or if he just couldn't feel the pain. They were almost all out of the bute Dr. Frankel had left for them.

"Ashleigh," Jonas called, leading Stardust into the aisle. "Look who's here."

"Stardust," Ashleigh breathed. The mare pricked her ears at the sound of Ashleigh's voice and began to paw at the aisle.

"Why don't you go out for a little ride?" Jonas suggested.

"I don't know . . ." Ashleigh hesitated. She wanted to spend the afternoon with Midnight, and she didn't feel much like riding, anyway. Just then her mother came in, leading Althea.

"I can groom Midnight for you," Jonas offered. "Stardust could use the exercise." Ashleigh knew Jonas was right—she hadn't ridden Stardust in a long time.

"Ashleigh, there's no point in having her here if you're not going to ride her," Mrs. Griffen reminded her as she walked by.

"All right, I'll take Stardust out," Ashleigh said, relenting. "But only if you're sure Midnight will be all right."

"Of course he'll be all right," Jonas said.

"Midnight will be fine," her mother assured her. "Would you mind taking Rory with you? He hasn't had much of a chance to ride Moe, and he's been dying to go out."

Ashleigh sighed, but her mother gave her an expectant look. "Oh, all right," she agreed.

Mrs. Griffen looked relieved. "Anyway, we've got a surprise for everyone when you get back, so don't be out for too long."

Ashleigh was curious. "A surprise? What is it?" she asked.

"Just you wait and see," Mrs. Griffen said, a twinkle in her eyes. "I'll go and get Rory."

Ashleigh laughed. She knew her mother liked to keep them all in suspense. She walked over to where Stardust stood in the crossties and began to curry the chestnut's dusty coat. Then she used a stiff body brush to whisk away all the excess dirt and hair, followed by a soft towel. Soon Stardust's coat was shining like a new penny. Out of the corner of her eye, Ashleigh could see Rory leading Moe out from his stall, all tacked up and ready to go.

"Hold on, Rory," she called to him. "I'll be tacked up in a sec. And then we'd better go, before it gets too dark."

Ashleigh helped Rory mount and then swung up into the saddle herself. So far, so good—Stardust hadn't done anything drastic. As they set off down the lanes, Stardust's head swung left and she began to sidestep. Ashleigh tried to straighten her out, but it wasn't until the mare decided for herself that she wanted to that she began to go forward properly. Stardust hadn't been ridden in over a week, so Ashleigh half expected the mare to bolt with her. She tried to ease the tension out of her arms as they walked on, and soon Stardust was moving forward, relaxed and on the bit.

Ashleigh looked at Rory. "Try to keep your hands by Moe's withers," she called.

Immediately Rory corrected himself. He was a fast learner and took his riding pretty seriously. Ashleigh smiled as she watched him concentrating. Rory and Moe looked cute together.

Now that they were away from the farm, Ashleigh was glad she had Rory with her for company. Concentrating on watching him meant that she couldn't worry about Midnight so much.

"Want to head up to the spring?" Ashleigh suggested.

"Great!" Rory cried.

As they rode on, Ashleigh began to relax. Ahead of them, the sun hovered brightly over the tops of the trees. Soon the days would be longer. Ashleigh was looking forward to seeing the bluegrass fields come alive in the spring sun. *Midnight will be going out in the paddocks by then,* she thought. *He'll be better soon.*

She snapped back to reality at the sight of a deer in the distance. "Did you see that, Rory? Come on, let's see if we can catch up to it!"

"Do you think we can?" Rory's eyes lit up.

"Well, we can try," Ashleigh said as she urged Stardust into a trot.

Ashleigh posted to the rise and fall of Stardust's gait, and Rory followed close behind them. Stardust was completely in control and responding willingly to Ashleigh's every aid. *Everything is going to be all right,* Ashleigh thought. *Midnight will get better, and Stardust and I will be friends.*

They trotted across the grass and into the trees, but the deer was out of sight.

"Come on," Ashleigh said, turning to Rory. "If we step up our pace, we can get to the spring and back before dinner."

"Great!" Rory exclaimed.

Ashleigh pressed Stardust into a canter and the mare moved forward eagerly, her ears pricked. Rory kept a safe distance behind them as they cantered along the path through the forest. When she saw the water ahead of her, Ashleigh sat back in the saddle and Stardust slowed down to an easy trot.

Again Ashleigh found herself riding on the path she and Mona had started out on when they'd found Lightning. *I've got to visit Hopewell,* Ashleigh reminded herself. She reached forward to stroke Stardust's neck. "And I'll tell Lightning all about how good you're being," she whispered to the mare.

Rory trotted up beside her. Moe was puffing, ready for a rest. "Moe wants to walk," Rory announced.

"Let's let the horses have a drink," Ashleigh suggested. "Then we should head back."

"Okay," Rory agreed, leading Moe over to the water. They lengthened their reins, and the two horses stretched out their necks to slurp noisily from the creek.

The sun was setting as they turned and walked leisurely back along the paths to the farm. Ashleigh hummed to herself. It had been a great ride, and Stardust had behaved flawlessly. Ashleigh reached forward to pat Stardust's neck. The mare gave a loud snort in response, and Ashleigh smiled. Mona was right— Stardust really was a clown.

As they rode down the grassy lanes, Ashleigh was surprised to see all of the horses still out. It looked as though her parents were running behind schedule.

"Come on, Rory," Ashleigh said. "Mom and Dad might need some help."

They trotted along the grass, slowing down to a walk as they neared the barn. Ashleigh jumped down from Stardust's back. She could hear troubled voices ahead of her. The panic rose in her throat. Midnight was the only horse in the barn.

Ashleigh put Stardust in crossties and raced to Midnight's stall. The door was open and her parents were inside.

"What's going on?" she cried out.

"It's all right. Midnight's fine now," Mrs. Griffen said, coming out of the stall and touching Ashleigh's arm. "The worst is over."

"What do you mean? What happened?" Ashleigh shrieked.

"Calm down, Ashleigh. He just scared himself, that's all," Mr. Griffen explained as he closed the stall door behind him. "We found him thrashing around in his stall. I've given him some ace, and he's better now."

"I've got to see him," Ashleigh cried, desperately trying to push past her mother's barring arm. "I should never have left him. I should have been here!"

"It's all right, Ashleigh," Mrs. Griffen repeated. "If

you'll just quiet down, you can go in and see him."

Ashleigh took a deep breath, feeling worried as she saw her parents exchange glances. What if Midnight had made his leg worse?

"Now," Mrs. Griffen said finally, "we're going back in the house to get dinner ready. You can have a few minutes with Midnight, but then you have to put Stardust away and come in to dinner."

Ashleigh rushed to Midnight's stall and looked in over his door. His head hung low facing the wall, his bad leg cocked as he stood in the straw. He didn't even look up at her. Ashleigh drew back the bolt and went inside. She felt the tears well up in her eyes as she reached up to stroke Midnight's neck. There was a heavy, drugged look in his eyes.

"Oh, Midnight." Ashleigh's lip quivered as she stroked his black mane with the lightest of touches. "I'm sorry I left you alone. You have to be good and keep still."

But of course Midnight didn't answer her, and it was with a heavy heart that Ashleigh let him go and closed the door to his stall. *I won't ride anymore*, Ashleigh vowed to herself. *Until Dr. Frankel comes next week, I'm going to spend all my free time keeping Midnight quiet.*

*   *   *

"So what's this surprise Mom was talking about?" Caroline asked, breaking the awkward silence as they sat down to dinner.

Ashleigh stared listlessly across the kitchen. All thoughts of her mother's surprise had flown out of her head after the scare with Midnight.

"Well, the Fontaines called this morning," Mrs. Griffen said brightly.

Ashleigh looked up. *How can everyone sound so cheerful?* she wondered.

Mrs. Griffen went on. "As you know, Wanderer's Quest is running in the Florida Derby at Gulfstream on Saturday. The Fontaines had some extra tickets—some deal with the Keeneland people here—and they invited us to go down there and watch her race. It's a step up in class for Quest and she probably won't win, but even so, it's an opportunity we don't want to miss. We'd just be there a night—we'd fly down to Fort Lauderdale after school on Friday and come back Saturday night. Jonas has said he can manage here without us."

"Wow! Way to go!" Rory cried, thrusting his fist in the air. Everyone laughed—everyone but Ashleigh.

"Will it be a big deal like the Kentucky Derby? Can we get dressed up?" Caroline asked, sounding impressed.

"Yes, we'll all have to get pretty dressed up." Mrs. Griffen assured her.

"Ashleigh, say something," Mr. Griffen begged. "This is supposed to be a treat for all of us."

Ashleigh looked at her father and then bowed her head. She had always been an avid fan of Wanderer's Quest, following her career from race to race. But now she found herself trying to think of a way to avoid going to Florida to watch Quest race. She just couldn't imagine leaving Midnight for all that time.

"Don't you want to go?" Mrs. Griffen demanded.

"I guess so," Ashleigh said. "But what about Midnight? Isn't the vet supposed to be coming?"

"Dr. Frankel will come on Sunday morning to see about Midnight. It's only a couple of days. Jonas will take good care of him," her father said.

Ashleigh pushed her food around on her plate while everyone chattered excitedly about Quest and the Florida Derby. How could her parents plan a trip like this when Midnight's future stood in the balance?

Finally they finished eating. Ashleigh pushed back her chair and took her plate over to the sink. She filled the sink with soapy water and began to do the dishes.

When the last bowl was dry, Ashleigh climbed the stairs to her bedroom. The lights were off and it was dark, but Ashleigh wanted it that way. Quickly she undressed and flopped onto her bed. Prince Charming mewed and jumped up beside her, kneading his paws into her arm. Ashleigh stroked his soft fur until the kitten began to purr noisily. Then Caroline opened the bedroom door.

"Hey, Ashleigh," Caroline said, plunking herself down on the end of Ashleigh's bed. "You know, you could have a been a little more enthusiastic about the trip to Florida."

Ashleigh didn't say anything.

"It hasn't been a very good time for any of us lately. Mom and Dad need a break," Caroline persisted. "They've been working so hard with the yearlings. Besides, we're really lucky the Fontaines are such generous owners. And it'll be warm," Caroline added.

"You're just glad you'll get to wear a new outfit," Ashleigh snapped. She couldn't help it, even though she was grateful to Caroline for being so nice to her since Midnight's injury.

"You can't get dragged down by all this, Ash," Caroline went on. "I know you feel worse about Midnight than any of us, but—"

"How would you know how I'm feeling?" Ashleigh burst out.

She turned over and buried her head in her pillow. Caroline left her alone, but it was a long while before Ashleigh fell asleep. Pictures of the terrified look in Midnight's eyes crowded her mind. Time was running out.

School did nothing to distract Ashleigh over the next few days. If anything, it made matters worse. She couldn't concentrate at all. Math, history, English . . . the classes flashed by in a blur, all merging into one. The days she was out sick had really put her behind.

"Come on, Ashleigh," Mona said, grabbing her friend's elbow as the lunch bell sounded around the school on Wednesday. "Jamie said she'll save us a place in the cafeteria."

Ashleigh nodded as Mona steered her down the hall. Kids pushed past them, jostling one another, and the noise of excited voices rose in the air.

Mona had been trying to lighten Ashleigh's spirits, but Ashleigh couldn't bring herself to be cheerful. Though she managed to put the food on her tray and walk toward Jamie at the table, she felt like a robot—as if she weren't really doing any of it herself. Even when she sat down to lunch and her friends' voices swam around her, she couldn't take part.

"Ashleigh, are you there? Come in, Ashleigh."

"What?" Ashleigh snapped to her senses at Jamie's question.

"I just asked how Midnight's feeling," Jamie explained.

"Fine, I guess," Ashleigh said. "He's still on a lot of bute, but at least it keeps him calm. The vet's coming on

Sunday, so we'll know more then." Ashleigh knew her words sounded hollow, and there was an uncomfortable silence.

"It must be costing your parents a fortune in medication," Jamie blurted out.

"Jamie!" Mona groaned.

Ashleigh felt a rush of anger. Jamie wasn't known for her tact, but even so, it wasn't something Ashleigh wanted to hear.

"Ashleigh's going down to see the Florida Derby at Gulfstream on Friday," Mona said, trying to change the subject. "Lucky," she added, glancing at Ashleigh.

But Ashleigh couldn't push Jamie's words out of her mind. Her parents *were* spending a lot of money on medications and the vet's visits. They couldn't support Midnight like this forever.

"Sorry, guys, I've got to go," Ashleigh muttered. She picked up her tray and hurried away from the table. *When will this day be over?* she thought.

"I know I've been taking this out on everybody—including you," Ashleigh said as she and Mona were riding home on the bus at the end of the day.

Mona shrugged. "That's okay, Ashleigh."

"It's just that what Jamie said was a little too close to the truth for comfort, that's all," Ashleigh explained. "I know my parents are really worrying about money, especially now that they can't sell Midnight. And it's true that Midnight's painkillers and stuff must be costing them a lot. If he has to be put down at the end of it, they'll have wasted all their money. And if he isn't put down, he may have to take expensive medicine his whole life."

"Come on, Ashleigh, you can't think like that," Mona said. "Your parents won't regret spending the money, and besides, you've got to be positive—he's not going to be put down. You said yourself he was starting to look a little better."

"I thought he was," Ashleigh said gloomily. "But Mom and Dad found him thrashing around in his stall again, and they had to tranquilize him. I'm just worried he's going to hurt himself even more when no one's watching. And now we're going to Florida. . . ."

"Listen, what are you doing this afternoon, Ash?" Mona asked as the bus sped around a turn. "Can I come to Edgardale and see how Midnight's doing? I haven't seen him since he hurt himself."

"Of course you can come and see him," Ashleigh said. "That would be great."

They rode along in comfortable silence for a while. The bus turned down a road near the Hopewell Center, and once again Ashleigh thought of Lightning.

"You know, Mona, I think I'm going to visit Lightning this week. I haven't seen her for so long, and every time I ride on that trail to the spring, I think about her," she said.

"I'll come with you if I can make it," Mona suggested.

The bus turned at a stop sign and roared down the road to Edgardale.

"Come on," Ashleigh said, jumping to her feet as the bus slowed to a stop in front of the long driveway leading to the farm. She made her way down to the front of the bus, and Mona followed her. The two girls climbed off and walked up the drive.

The barn was a hive of activity as they walked into the aisle. Ashleigh's parents were there with Jonas and Rory—even Caroline had somehow managed to get home ahead of Ashleigh.

"Hi, Mona." Mrs. Griffen smiled. "We haven't seen you around here in a while."

"How's Midnight been today?" Ashleigh asked anxiously, already heading for the yearling's stall.

"Pretty quiet," Mrs. Griffen called as the two girls rushed off down the aisle.

"Hello there, my boy," Ashleigh whispered as she drew back the bolt to his stall. Midnight snorted and hobbled forward to greet them. "How are you feeling, Midnight?"

Mona followed Ashleigh into the stall and patted Midnight's neck. He craned his neck around, sniffing at

Mona's sweatshirt. The yearling's eyes were bright, and Ashleigh was glad to see him taking an interest in things again.

"Well, he looks pretty happy," Mona said. "If it weren't for the cast, I'd never know anything was wrong."

Ashleigh was thrilled. "Do you really think so, Mona?" she asked happily.

"He looks great, Ashleigh," Mona insisted.

Ashleigh grinned. "Do you want to help me groom him?"

"Sure," Mona said.

"Good. Now, did you hear that, Midnight?" Ashleigh said, unfastening Midnight's New Zealand rug. "Mona thinks you look great. So you just keep it up."

Ashleigh picked up a body brush, and they began to groom Midnight's black coat. While Mona combed his forelock, Ashleigh started on his back, working toward his muscular hindquarters and down his back legs. When she reached the plaster cast, she frowned. Mona might think Midnight looked good, but everything depended on Dr. Frankel's visit on Sunday.

7

"I can't wait for Derby Day," Caroline said at breakfast on Thursday.

The Griffens were flying to Florida the next day, and Ashleigh had been dreading it all week.

"Ashleigh," her father said brightly, "I guess you didn't hear. We were talking about Quest's race in Florida on Saturday."

"Yes, I heard, and I wish we weren't going," Ashleigh said before she could stop herself. There was an awkward silence as everyone studied her.

"What do you mean?" her father asked, stirring his coffee.

"Just that," Ashleigh answered, fingering her toast. "I don't want to go."

Mr. Griffen put his spoon down. "But Ashleigh," he said, "this is a great treat. The Fontaines are so happy with Quest that they're being extremely generous toward us. We should be honored that—"

"Don't you understand?" Ashleigh interrupted, looking her father dead in the eye. "I can't believe you want me to watch Midnight's half-sister run when we know he'll never be able to race!"

"Midnight's accident has been painful for all of us," her father said firmly. "This trip will give us time to get away from it all. I expect you to have a bag packed and ready before you leave for school tomorrow."

Ashleigh knew there was no point in arguing, but she couldn't imagine leaving Midnight, even for a night. Anything might happen if she wasn't watching him. What good would she be to the yearling if she was in Florida?

Ashleigh stood up and slung her backpack on her shoulder.

"I'm going to drop by Hopewell on the way home from school today," she said. "I need to see Lightning."

"All right," her mother replied. "Say hello to her for me. And call us when you're ready to be picked up."

"Fine," Ashleigh said, and headed off for school.

When Ashleigh's bus reached the road that was just a few minutes' walk from Hopewell, she said good-bye to Mona and asked the driver to let her off. Mona had a jumping lesson scheduled for that afternoon, so she couldn't join Ashleigh.

As Ashleigh made her way up the tree-lined drive that led to Hopewell, she thought back to the first time she had visited the place. It seemed so long ago now, though only a few months had passed. Ashleigh felt ashamed that she'd waited so long to visit Lightning again, but now it seemed like the only thing that might make her feel better.

Ahead of her was the large ivy-covered house that served as a temporary home for the children. Two immaculate white barns lay behind it, with white-fenced paddocks stretching as far as the eye could see. The sound of cantering hooves filled the air. Ashleigh stepped up her pace and walked around the first barn. She smiled as she saw Lightning going around the outdoor ring. Ashleigh recognized the Hopewell patient on Lightning's back as Kyle, a wheelchair-bound boy about Rory's age.

A group of children were gathered, watching. Ashleigh stood back for a moment, reluctant to intrude. She was pleased to see the smiles on their faces. They were all so brave dealing with their illnesses. Ashleigh knew, just as she had that first day, that letting Lightning come to live there had been the right choice. The center had lots of animals, but Lightning was their first horse, and the pleasure that the mare could give these kids was priceless.

Ashleigh watched as Kyle changed rein across the

diagonal and did a neat figure eight. Lightning was a nice horse, and Kyle was riding her well—heels down, shoulders straight, eyes fixed ahead in concentration. A slim, red-haired woman in jeans was giving instructions from the rail. It was Sally, the center's physical therapist and horse person.

"Bring her to a halt now, Kyle, and try reining back," Sally called.

Ashleigh watched Kyle slow Lightning down to an even halt in the center of the ring and rein back with ease. Just at that moment Ashleigh must have caught Lightning's eye, because the white mare let out a loud whinny.

"Ashleigh!" Sally waved.

Ashleigh waved back, feeling her heart constrict as she realized how much she'd missed Lightning.

Kyle saw Ashleigh and dropped the reins, waving furiously, "Look, no hands!" he called, laughing. Lightning didn't flinch.

"All right, Kyle, that was very good," Sally said as she walked into the center of the ring. "But it's your dinnertime now, so I'll put Lightning away for you."

"Aw." Kyle looked disappointed, but he didn't argue. Sally helped him down into his wheelchair, and Kyle rolled the chair off across the grass to join the other kids.

Sally led Lightning over to Ashleigh. "I thought you'd

forgotten us now that Kira's back home," she said, smiling.

"I know, I should have come before this," Ashleigh admitted, embarrassed. "So much has been happening at Edgardale, I just haven't had a chance."

"Well, as you can see, she's doing just fine," Sally said. "How are you, anyway?"

"Okay, I guess," Ashleigh said, leaning over the railing to stroke the white mare's nose. "I've missed you, girl," she whispered. She turned back to Sally and said, "She looks great."

"Well, I try to give her the best care I can now that Kira's gone home," Sally said, smiling wistfully. "But tell me, Ashleigh—is something not right with you?" she asked, touching Ashleigh's shoulder.

Suddenly, seeing Lightning and Sally's friendly smile were too much for Ashleigh, and the tears started streaming down her face. Sally didn't say anything. She just stood there stroking Ashleigh's hair.

"Come on, you can help me put Lightning away for the night," Sally suggested finally. "So how's the new horse—Stardust, right?" she asked as she led Lightning off to the barn.

"She's fine," Ashleigh said, following them. One of the barn cats came and rubbed against her legs. Ashleigh bent down to pet it. She didn't know how she was going to explain everything to Sally.

Sally untacked Lightning, and Ashleigh began to brush her. When she was clean, Ashleigh led the white mare into her stall while Sally filled her hay net.

"Now," Sally said, tying the hay net up, "why don't I drive you home, and you can tell me all about it?"

"Thanks," Ashleigh said. Sally stood back to wait as Ashleigh turned to hug Lightning good-bye. The white mare nudged her chest, and Ashleigh rearranged her forelock. "Bye, girl," Ashleigh whispered. "I'll be back soon."

"We owe you so much for giving us Lightning," Sally said as they made their way out of the barn. "I know it was difficult for you. I want to help if I can."

"I guess that's part of why I didn't come for a while. It *is* hard to come here and see Lightning, and then leave her behind," Ashleigh admitted as they walked to Sally's station wagon. "Stardust and I didn't get along very well in the beginning, and . . . oh, I don't know." Ashleigh felt confused. She hadn't even told Sally about Midnight yet, and she was already getting upset.

"Come on," Sally said, opening the car door. "Hop in. I'll drive slowly, and you can start at the beginning."

Ashleigh got in the passenger side and buckled her seat belt. Sally revved the engine and they started down the drive. Ashleigh took a deep breath. "I don't know if you remember, but last year when one of the brood-mares was sick, Rory and I nursed her foal," she began.

"Yes, wasn't he called Tonka?" Sally asked.

"That's right—you have a good memory. He was registered as Midnight Wanderer at the beginning of the year, so I've been calling him Midnight." Ashleigh took a deep breath. "Anyway, a couple of weekends ago, there was an accident in the paddock. Midnight was fighting with one of the other yearlings. My sister, Caroline, thought we should stop them, but I told her not to, and then Midnight got hurt. He reared up and landed badly and he . . . he broke the cannon bone in his right hind leg."

"What! But is he all right?" Sally demanded, looking shocked.

Ashleigh couldn't contain herself any longer. "No, he's not all right!" she cried. "The vet thought we should put him down, but I wouldn't let him. Mom and Dad convinced him to put Midnight in a cast, and he said we could have two weeks to see if the bone would start to heal." Ashleigh was speaking quickly, through her tears. "But it's been almost two weeks—the vet's coming back on Sunday. Midnight has been on tons of bute, and I've been spending all my free time with him, trying to keep him quiet. But now my parents are taking us to Gulf-stream, to the races. I won't be able to watch Midnight. I don't know what to do—I don't want to go!"

"Ashleigh," Sally said slowly, as if she was choosing each word carefully, "I'm sure you've done everything in your power to help Midnight. If his leg is meant to heal, it will. I'm sure the vet knows what he's doing—he only wants what's best for the horse."

"The vet said he'll never race. But that doesn't matter—we could keep him as a pleasure horse," Ashleigh explained. "Midnight was the most valuable of all our yearlings. I know Mom and Dad are worried about money, too," she added.

"But about this race in Florida," Sally intervened. "You love racing. I know you don't want to leave Midnight, but I think you'll enjoy yourself at Gulfstream—it sounds like fun."

"Maybe." Ashleigh nodded slowly. "But ever since Midnight got hurt I haven't felt like doing anything."

Sally put her hand on Ashleigh's shoulder. "And what about Stardust? Haven't you been riding?"

"I've only ridden once since Midnight hurt himself," Ashleigh admitted. "I just can't leave him."

"Ashleigh, horrible accidents happen all the time, but you can't give up the things you love because of them. Stardust needs you—who's going to ride her if you're not going to do it?"

"I don't know," Ashleigh mumbled. "I guess I haven't told you everything. See, before Midnight's accident things weren't going that well with Stardust," she explained. "Whenever I took her out, she'd hardly listen. I'd ask her to do one thing, and she'd do something else. And now that I've sort of stopped riding her, I haven't really missed it. I mean, Stardust and I never clicked. Maybe I should just give up while I can."

"Ashleigh Griffen," Sally said with a frown, "are you the same girl who made Lightning the horse she is today? I can't believe you're thinking of giving in without putting up a fight. Of course Stardust's difficult—wouldn't you be if you'd gone through what she has? It's going to be a while before she trusts anyone again, but you're nearly there. All that training you've put in with her—don't waste it. She's a beautiful horse. Get her going right and she'll be your wonder horse."

A picture of the pretty copper-colored mare flashed through Ashleigh's mind. "Maybe you're right," she said reluctantly.

"I understand it can be a little scary if she's acting up, but horses know when something's bothering a rider, so you've got to be firm. If she knows she's intimidating you, she'll take advantage," Sally instructed.

"But how can I work with her if she doesn't trust me?" Ashleigh asked.

"If you trust her, she'll trust you," Sally said. "It's the same with friends. You don't get trust by doing nothing; you have to earn it. I think you should give Stardust a chance. I know this thing with Midnight has taken a lot out of you, but Stardust needs you, too, maybe even more than Midnight."

Ashleigh thought about it. Sally might be right. Maybe she and Stardust did need to spend more time getting to know each other. But she had promised not to leave Midnight. Stardust would have to wait.

Sally raised her eyebrows. "Whatever you decide, do one thing for me," she said.

"What?" Ashleigh asked, studying Sally's profile.

"Enjoy yourself at Gulfstream. I know it's hard, but worrying won't get you anywhere. Who knows what the vet will say when you come back? Maybe Midnight's doing better than you think."

Ashleigh nodded her response and gazed out the window. They were pulling into Edgardale, and she could see the horses all lined up by the paddock gates as they waited to be brought in for their evening feed.

"Now remember, you can come back and visit us anytime," Sally said, stopping the car.

"Thanks for everything, Sally," Ashleigh said as she got out. "I feel a lot better," she added, and she meant it.

"I hope so," Sally said, smiling. She backed the car up and rolled her window down. "Have fun in Florida!"

Ashleigh waved. "I will!" she called.

8

"Fasten your seat belts and prepare for landing," the pilot's voice announced over the loudspeaker. Ashleigh pulled a face and clutched her armrest. It was only two hours from Lexington's airport to Fort Lauderdale, but she didn't like flying. Somehow being airborne was much more frightening than riding!

Ashleigh shut her eyes tight as the plane touched down and rolled to a stop at the gate. As the Griffens gathered up their belongings and made their way off the aircraft, Ashleigh took a deep breath. She was in Florida, far from Midnight. There was no turning back.

She had spent an hour with the yearling that morning before school and hated to leave him, but she had no choice. Now, as Ashleigh emerged from the airport terminal, the warm breeze bathed her face and she squinted in the late afternoon sunlight. It was still winter in Kentucky, but it felt like summer in Florida. *Maybe Sally's right,* Ashleigh thought. It might be good to get away, and seeing Quest race would be fun.

Soon Ashleigh and her family were in a taxi, flying down the freeway. They were staying in a motel on the outskirts of Fort Lauderdale, a half hour's drive from Gulfstream Park.

As they pulled into the parking lot Caroline let out a yell. "Great! It's even got a swimming pool!" she cried.

"Not that you're going to have much time to use it," Mr. Griffen said with a chuckle. "We'll be watching the races tomorrow."

"Still," Caroline cried, "we've got all night to go for a swim. Come on, Ash, race you there!"

Ashleigh laughed and jumped out of the cab. "Last one in is a rotten egg!"

The Griffens got to Gulfstream Park a couple of hours before the first race was due to start, so they could soak up the atmosphere at the track. The Florida Derby was the third race of the day, and as a result they had some time to go until Quest would run.

As they walked through the main gates a band was already striking up a tune, and brightly colored flags flapped in the breeze. Ashleigh had never been to a Florida track, and she was surprised at how different it was from Kentucky. With the heat and the sound of steel drums playing, there was a tropical feel to Gulfstream.

Ashleigh could already feel her clothes sticking to her skin, and she hoped the weather wouldn't keep Quest from running well. The mare already had a hard enough task ahead of her. Although Quest had run in grade one stakes races before, this one had a purse of $750,000.

"Ashleigh, I know you're dying to get to the backside, but we ought to go find the Fontaines first and let them know we're here," Mr. Griffen said.

"All right," Ashleigh agreed with a nod.

The Griffens walked across the grounds behind the grandstand, then made their way up the escalators toward the private boxes.

"Number thirty," Mr. Griffen said, looking at the piece of paper in his hands. "That's where we'll find them."

After walking through a maze of tunnels and corridors behind the stands, the Griffens soon found themselves knocking on the door of the Fontaines' box.

"Derek, Elaine." Mr. Fontaine extended a welcoming hand as the Griffens walked into the box. He was wearing a suit—dressed for the winner's circle, just in case.

Mrs. Fontaine took Ashleigh's shoulders in her gloved hands and squeezed them. "And of course here's Ashleigh," she said, beaming. Then she turned to Ashleigh's sister. "And lovely Caroline," she said, hugging

Caroline. Ashleigh liked the Fontaines; they were full of warm southern hospitality.

"How you doin', little fella?" Mr. Fontaine asked, shaking Rory's hand. "My, you're growing, young man!" Rory, who was wearing his best clothes, squirmed uncomfortably.

"Let me introduce our grandson, Christopher." Mr. Fontaine indicated the good-looking teenage boy at his side. Ashleigh raised her eyebrows as she saw Caroline preen herself and smile, her blue eyes flashing.

"Dad," Rory said, tugging at his father's sleeve, "I want to see the horses."

"In a minute," Mr. Griffen answered him.

"I'll take him," Ashleigh offered. "If it's okay."

"All right, go on." Mr. Griffen smiled. "But don't let Rory out of your sight, and come back before the first race. It's a great view from up here."

"You're right," Ashleigh agreed, glancing briefly over the balcony at the track below. The white rails shone brightly in the sun, and the red finish post stood out as bold as anything.

There were two tracks at Gulfstream, one dirt and one turf. The Derby was to be run on dirt, but the grass oval inside it was a lush emerald green, lined with landscaped flower beds, making a spectacular sight. There was a lake in the middle of the track, too, with pink flamingos wading gracefully in it.

"Do you want to come, Caro?" Ashleigh asked her sister as she took Rory's hand.

"I think I'll stay here," Caroline answered, glancing out of the corner of her eye at Christopher. Ashleigh smiled. Caroline was so predictable.

"Come on, Rory." Ashleigh led her little brother down the grandstand steps and out onto the grounds. "Let's go and see Quest, okay?"

"Good idea, Ash. Hey, do you think she'll recognize us?" he asked.

"I doubt it, Rory," Ashleigh said. "She's grown up a lot since she lived at Edgardale."

Quest had been an even-tempered, beautiful filly, just like Midnight. It had been clear right from the start that she would be a champion. But Ashleigh was glad that the Fontaines owned her now. They had only a few racehorses, and they really cared about them all.

The stands were filling up as Ashleigh and Rory headed for the backside. There were a lot of very fancy people there, too—women in brightly colored outfits of all kinds, and smartly dressed men in suits. Everything smelled of money. That was hardly surprising—this was Derby day, the most important day of the Florida racing calendar.

It didn't take Ashleigh and Rory long to reach the backside. Grooms led sheeted horses over the gravel paths, and reporters were setting up along with their camera crews. Ashleigh found the shedrow where Quest was stabled. She felt a sharp pain in her chest as she recognized the black mare looking out over one of the stall doors. With her coal-black nose and intelligent brown eyes, she looked so much like Midnight it hurt. *I wonder what Midnight's doing right now,* Ashleigh thought.

"There she is, Rory," Ashleigh said, pointing at the black mare as a lump formed in her throat.

"I see her!" Rory cried excitedly. "Let's get closer."

At that moment the groom led Quest out of her stall and removed her sheet for a press photograph. Quest's coat was so shiny it looked like black satin. She really was a magnificent animal, with lovely sloping shoulders, long, straight legs, and massive hindquarters.

"Let's go," Ashleigh said as the groom put the mare back into her stall. "Quest has to get ready for her race. We don't want to bother her. Let's go see some of the other horses."

They passed chestnuts and bays, grays and blacks. Every one of the Thoroughbreds was immaculately turned out—all ready for the races ahead of them.

"We should get back," Ashleigh said finally. "The first race is about to start."

"Do we have to?" Rory groaned.

"Come on. I know you want to see the races," Ashleigh said with a laugh.

"How did the horses look, Ashleigh?" Mrs. Fontaine

greeted them when they returned to the box.

"Great. We saw Quest, and she looked beautiful," Ashleigh breathed, feeling a little sad. Mr. Griffen put his hand on Ashleigh's shoulder, as if he knew she was thinking about Midnight.

"Quest's been putting in some good times," Mrs. Fontaine said. "But we're not holding out too much hope—there are some fine horses in this race."

"Who's the favorite?" Ashleigh asked, sitting down.

"I should think it's Supreme Sound," her father said. "He's won all of his races to date. We're going to stay up here till Quest's race, then we'll go down to the walking ring to watch her."

"All right," Ashleigh nodded.

The first two races—a grade two stakes and a grade three handicap—seemed to fly by, with both favorites leading from post to wire. Ashleigh had forgotten the thrill that she felt on the track as she watched the horses galloping down to the finish. The speed, the power, the will to win . . . nothing could beat that.

Before the Derby, the entrants were exhibited in the walking ring. Each horse was led around the outside of the ring so that the spectators could size up their prospects before placing their bets. Caroline had managed to wangle a place in the ring with Ashleigh's parents and the Fontaines, while Ashleigh and Rory soaked up the atmosphere on the rail.

Ashleigh glanced at the odds board. Supreme Sound was the even-money favorite, then Silver Eagle at 3–1, and Scent of Success at 8–1. Quest was the joint outsider of the field at 30–1, but Ashleigh had faith. She had given her mother two dollars to bet on her.

Ashleigh had her eyes fixed on Quest as the horses made their way around the paddock. The black mare pranced gaily around the ring, looking every inch a champion. Each step that she took seemed to command attention. Her ears were pricked, her eyes were alert, and she looked completely at ease. She was a true Wanderer mare, and again Ashleigh was reminded of Midnight.

Now the jockeys were walking into the middle of the ring and talking to the owners. They made a fine spectacle in their brightly colored silks. Then the race announcer called, "Riders up." Quest was led into the center of the ring and her jockey was given a leg up into the saddle. Then they walked down to the track, where their pony escorts led them off in the post parade.

Ashleigh's family and the Fontaines made their way back to their seats. The atmosphere in the box was silent and tense. Ashleigh could hardly contain herself as she watched the horses begin to load into the starting gate. The race was a mile and an eighth—just over a full circuit. She fiddled with the binoculars she'd been given for her birthday the year before, waiting impatiently for the start of the race. Peering through them, she could see the handlers lead each horse into the gate.

Quest went in quietly. She had an inside draw—a good slot, since it meant she would save ground around the turns. Ashleigh watched Supreme Sound being loaded. The favorite was putting up a fight, and the other horses were getting jumpy. Finally they put a hood over Supreme Sound's eyes and he walked in. Ashleigh raised her binoculars to her eyes. They were all in, ready for the start.

The gates opened, and the horses were away for the running of the Florida Derby. Ashleigh's eyes were trained on Quest as her jockey vied for position and tucked the mare into fourth place on the rail. Ashleigh listened for the announcer's call.

"And it's Supreme Sound who's kicked clear of the pack by three lengths. Racing quickly in the red is Further Outlook. Chasing them in third is Silver Eagle. Then it's Wanderer's Quest behind in fourth. . . ."

There was a stream of names that Ashleigh didn't listen to. As they raced through the clubhouse turn her eyes were keenly focused on one horse—Quest, who was running boldly. The front-runners were setting a blazing pace, but Quest wasn't going to let them get away from her.

"Now they're through the first eighth of a mile. Conqueror is the back marker of the field. Supreme Sound has increased her gap to four lengths from Further Outlook."

"Hang in there, Quest," Ashleigh said to herself, lifting her binoculars to her eyes as the field thundered into the backstretch.

"Supreme Sound is on the inside, then Further Outlook," the announcer called. "Silver Eagle is moving up fast in the pink silks. Half a length back is Wanderer's Quest. They're setting a good pace now. Supreme Sound is being tracked by Further Outlook, who's narrowed the gap to a length. Then it's half a length back to Silver Eagle, and another half a length to Wanderer's Quest. They've moved away from the rest of the field." The horses galloped along the approach to the far turn.

"Come on, Quest. Hurry up!" Ashleigh cried.

Now that the horses were running full out in the middle of the race, Ashleigh forgot all her troubles and started cheering wholeheartedly for Wanderer's Quest. She dropped her binoculars and gripped her father's elbow. There was only three-eighths of a mile left to go. Quest was still up there, but she was some three lengths off the lead. Did she have anything left?

Ashleigh craned her neck to see as they came into the top of the homestretch. Silver Eagle had quickened the pace and moved up to join Further Outlook and Supreme Sound. Wanderer's Quest wasn't far behind, but she was boxed in and there was nowhere left for her to go. Ashleigh hardly dared to look, let alone breathe.

"And Wanderer's Quest is pulling wide!" the announcer called excitedly. "Silver Eagle is dropping away. And here comes Wanderer's Quest now, with a bold run on the stand side!"

Quest was running her heart out—neck stretched out, powerful legs churning, her black coat covered in lather—doing what she was bred to do.

"Come on, girl!" Ashleigh screamed, nearly making herself hoarse. Suddenly nothing else mattered but the race. Quest just had to win. Ashleigh jumped up and down on the spot. The black mare was a length off the leader now, but they were at the sixteenth pole and the wire was getting nearer and nearer.

"Go, Quest, go!" Ashleigh shouted, over and over.

"Supreme Sound still has the edge, but Wanderer's Quest is coming to challenge the lead. These two have settled down to fight it out. And it's Wanderer's Quest and Supreme Sound racing neck and neck—too close to call! Stand by for photo!"

The infield board flashed the word *photo*.

Ashleigh turned to her parents. "Did Quest get it?" she asked breathlessly.

The two lead horses circled in front of the wire, awaiting the announcement. It had been so close.

"I don't know," her father answered doubtfully. "It was too close to tell."

The Fontaines excused themselves to find their trainer down at the rail. Ashleigh paced up and down, feeling a mixture of emotions. It had been a fantastic race, but seeing how Quest had eaten up the track as she zoomed to the finish had made Ashleigh wonder about Midnight. He would love to gallop like that; as with Quest, racing was in his blood. But Midnight could never gallop again, and he'd never be able to race like Quest. *Could he still be happy?* Ashleigh wondered.

Tension filled the stands as they waited for the results of the photo. When the infield board flashed Quest's number in first place, Ashleigh could hardly believe it.

"She did it! She did it!" Ashleigh cried, unable to hold back the tears that cascaded down her cheeks. "Quest won the Florida Derby!"

Her parents looked as though they would burst with pride. "I can't believe one of our babies has won," Mrs. Griffen said, thunderstruck.

"I never thought she'd do it," Mr. Griffen said, looking equally shocked.

"Did you have any money on her, Mom?" Ashleigh asked breathlessly.

"I sure did." Mrs. Griffen's eyes sparkled. "And your two dollars is worth a little more now," she added.

Quest's trainer led the black mare into the winner's circle. Her jockey was handed a huge rosette, and the Fontaines went forward to collect their trophy. Swept up in the thrill of Quest's race, Ashleigh stood and joined in the applause. *Midnight,* Ashleigh thought, *if you could see your big sister now, you'd be so proud.*

The mare stood for her pictures, tossing her elegant black head and snorting for the cameras. Again Ashleigh thought of Midnight. He would never stand where Quest was standing now, the proud winner of a race. But what sort of fate *would* he have?

It would all be decided the next day, when the vet returned to Edgardale.

9

"There, Midnight," Ashleigh said, as she brushed a stray bit of straw from the yearling's black forelock. "What a handsome boy you are."

Ashleigh had risen early that morning with a sense of dread. The day of Dr. Frankel's visit had loomed like a black cloud on her calendar, and now it was here. The night before, she had dashed straight to the barn just as soon as they arrived from the airport. She spent an hour grooming Midnight and telling the black horse all about his wonderful half-sister. Jonas had kept a close eye on him while they were gone, and Midnight seemed to be in good spirits.

Now, as Dr. Frankel stood beside her parents and looked in over Midnight's door, Ashleigh was certain he'd be pleased with what he saw. Midnight's coat gleamed like coal, his ears were pricked, and his eyes were shining. Except for the cast, he was the complete picture of health.

"He is okay, isn't he?" Ashleigh asked. "He's going to be all right?" All of a sudden she felt very shaky.

"Well, he seems pretty calm, and he looks magnificent," Dr. Frankel said. "You've done a fantastic job of looking after him, Ashleigh."

Ashleigh heard the unspoken concern in the vet's voice. She waited for him to continue.

"I can't give you a complete report, though, until I've taken X rays," Dr. Frankel explained.

"Oh," Ashleigh said, disappointed. She hadn't thought about X rays. Somehow she'd imagined that Dr. Frankel would give them a verdict right then and there. "But the X rays will show that everything's all right, won't they? You said he looks calm—he can't be in much pain," she said hopefully.

Dr. Frankel looked serious. "But that's no indication as to how the bone is knitting. And I know he's on a lot of bute."

"We finished the supply you left," Mr. Griffen joined in. "We had to buy more."

"Look," Dr. Frankel said. "I don't want to say anything until I've got the results of the X rays. I know you're anxious, so I'll take them up to the lab myself and call you this afternoon."

Ashleigh didn't budge.

"Now, this will take a while," Dr. Frankel went on. "If your father will hold him, I can get the ball rolling. The rest of you go on and have your lunch. Don't worry, I'll call from the lab just as soon as I can."

Ashleigh nodded, feeling a lump rise in her throat. Although Dr. Frankel had said that he and her father would handle the exam, she was reluctant to leave Midnight.

"Ashleigh," Mrs. Griffen called, raising her eyebrows. "Come on."

"All right," Ashleigh said, swallowing nervously. As hard as it was to leave, she knew Midnight was in capable hands.

With a choking feeling, she hurried across the drive to the house. Stardust nickered to her from the paddock, but Ashleigh ignored her and kept on walking.

Caroline was busy preparing lunch when Ashleigh pushed back the screen door.

"Dr. Frankel's taking some X rays," Ashleigh explained. "He's going to take them up to the lab and call us as soon as he sees them."

"I'm sure they'll show Midnight's doing fine," Caroline said. She gave Ashleigh a little hug. "Try not to worry."

"Can I do something to help, Caro?" Ashleigh offered, welcoming any distraction.

"You could set the table," Caroline suggested.

Ashleigh took a stack of plates out of the cupboard. She filled three glasses with milk and ripped paper towels off the roll for napkins. Then she sat down at the table, nervously folding the paper towels in halves, then quarters, then eighths, over and over, until the paper began to tear. Outside, she heard Dr. Frankel's Bronco start up and drive out of the yard. He was off with Midnight's future in his hands, and all she could do was wait.

"What time did he say he'd call?" Ashleigh asked her parents for the umpteenth time, pushing her sandwich around on her plate.

"Oh, Ashleigh, don't start again," Mr. Griffen said in exasperation. "You know as well as I do that Dr. Frankel said he'd call as soon as he knows anything."

"But it's been over an hour," Ashleigh said.

Every passing minute seemed like an eternity to her. The phone had already rung twice, and both times Ashleigh had jumped to her feet. The first call was from Mona, asking for news, and the second call was from Rory. Mrs. Griffen had sent him off to a friend's house for the day, but he was as desperate as Ashleigh to know Midnight's fate.

Now, as the four of them sat mulling over their lunch, there was an uncomfortable silence. Mr. Griffen was the first one to push his plate of food aside.

"I don't think I feel like anything more," he said.

"Me neither," Ashleigh agreed.

"Come on, you two, you've got to eat," Mrs. Griffen urged. "I don't know what I'm going to do if—" But her voice broke off as they heard the sound of a car in the yard.

"That sounds like Dr. Frankel," Mr. Griffen said, frowning.

Ashleigh jumped to her feet, her thoughts racing. "Why did he come back again?" she cried. "He said he'd call."

"I don't know," Mr. Griffen said, looking worried.

Ashleigh pushed her chair away, knocking it to the floor in her effort to get to the door. She didn't have to go very far—Dr. Frankel was already standing on the porch. Ashleigh knew by the look on his face that something was wrong.

"Tell us what you found," Mr. Griffen said, walking up behind Ashleigh.

"Well," Dr. Frankel said, and took a deep breath. "The X rays weren't good. The fracture hasn't improved at all. In fact, it's a little worse. The bone doesn't seem to be knitting, and I'm afraid he has a secondary infection despite the antibiotics we've given him."

Ashleigh felt dizzy. Dr. Frankel's face swam in front of her. In one split second, her whole world came crashing down around her.

"I know how hard it is to keep young horses quiet, so

you mustn't blame yourselves for this. Midnight's being very brave," Dr. Frankel said seriously. "But you have to think of what's best for him and yourselves. If you keep him alive, it would only take a little knock for him to be back to square one. He'd definitely have to be on medication for the rest of his life, he'd always feel some pain, and he'd probably never walk comfortably, let alone gallop."

"But—" Ashleigh was speechless. She turned to look at her parents. Their shoulders were slumped in defeat, but Ashleigh wasn't ready to give up.

"He could just be a pleasure horse—we knew he wouldn't be able to race," she insisted. "We could keep him here. I'll take care of him and make sure he doesn't hurt himself. We could put him out to stud. . . ." She had to try, but the words sounded confused, even to her own ears.

"You can't watch him night and day, Ashleigh," Mr. Griffen said, his expression sad. "And you can't stop him from wanting to gallop."

"What do you mean? What are you saying?" Ashleigh cried.

"This isn't a little Shetland pony we're talking about, Ashleigh," Mrs. Griffen put in. "Midnight was bred to be a racehorse."

"He'll be all right, Mom. You could ride him . . . you and Dad," Ashleigh said, desperately trying to win them over.

"We've got to listen to what Dr. Frankel is saying," Mrs. Griffen said. "We knew Midnight's chances of recovery were slim." She touched Ashleigh's arm, and Ashleigh flinched. "We have to think of what's best for the horse."

"So you're saying you're going to put him down?" Ashleigh could barely get the words out.

"I'm going to be straight with you," Dr. Frankel said, catching Ashleigh's eye. "Yes, I recommend putting Midnight down."

"It would be the kindest thing," her mother said hesitantly.

Ashleigh couldn't listen to another word. She turned and fled through the kitchen, up the stairs, and straight to her bedroom, slamming the door shut behind her. Breathless, she stood with her back to the door, trying to take it all in. This was all happening so quickly, and she needed time to think. She wasn't prepared.

Ashleigh crossed the room and sat on her bed, in such a state of shock that she couldn't even cry. She stared into space. A few minutes later there was a knock on the door.

"Ashleigh, can I come in?" her mother called. "I need to talk to you. Dr. Frankel's gone over to the barn with your father. Of course you know what the vet thinks we need to do, but I wanted to talk to you first." Mrs. Griffen pushed open the door and stood looking down at Ashleigh.

"I don't know why you're even bothering to include me," Ashleigh cried. "It sounds like you've decided to put Midnight down anyway. How can you be so mean? All you care about is the money you'd have to spend on his medicine!" Ashleigh said the most hurtful thing that came into her head. Even as she said it she knew how ridiculous it sounded—her parents gave up everything for their horses.

"Now you know that's not fair," Mrs. Griffen said, but her voice was gentle.

"How can you just give up on him?" Ashleigh demanded, her words catching in her throat.

"Oh, Ashleigh," Mrs. Griffen said, her eyes sympathetic. "You've done a wonderful job of looking after Midnight. Just seeing the way he looks at you is heartbreaking."

Ashleigh could take it no more. At the thought of Midnight's sweet face, she burst into tears.

Mrs. Griffen sat down on the bed beside her daughter. "Dr. Frankel was probably right all along. It might have been better to put him down right away, but we wanted to give him a chance. We wanted to believe that the leg might start to heal," she explained. "I'm sorry we put you through all this."

"You didn't put me through it," Ashleigh insisted. "I did. I was the one who asked you to let me try."

Mrs. Griffen took a deep breath. "If you love Midnight, and I know you do, then I know you'll want to do the best thing for him, too," she said.

"I can't," Ashleigh said, the tears streaming down her face. "I feel so bad." Everything that her mother was saying made sense, but Ashleigh didn't want to hear it. Every day Midnight had become dearer and dearer to her, and none of this would have happened if she had done something to prevent it in the first place.

"We have to make a decision," her mother went on. "And sometimes the best choice isn't always the easiest one to make. I had something bad like this happen to me when I was about your age—"

"Please, I don't want to hear about it," Ashleigh cried, cutting her mother off. "Nothing could be worse than this!"

"Ashleigh," her mother said quietly, trying to calm her, "your father and Dr. Frankel are waiting outside. I have to go back and tell them what we've agreed. A life of pain isn't really a good life. Don't you think it's for the best to put him down—for his sake?"

"No," Ashleigh cried out, but she knew she was wrong. "I mean," she said, and took a deep breath, "yes." The word came out in a whisper.

"Are you sure?" Mrs. Griffen said.

"Yes, I know you're right," Ashleigh said, staring blindly through her tears. "I don't want him to be in pain."

Her mother stood up to get a tissue from the box on Caroline's bureau. She handed it to Ashleigh, and Ashleigh blew her nose.

"It's for the best," her mother repeated.

But just then Ashleigh had a horrible thought. "Where will you do it?" she cried. "You won't send him away, will you? This is the only home he's ever known," she sobbed, gulping for breath. "It wouldn't be right for him to go anywhere else."

"No, we'll bury him on the farm." Mrs. Griffen said, her voice barely a whisper. She turned away and looked out the window, and Ashleigh could see that her mother was fighting back the tears.

"How are we going to tell Rory?" Ashleigh demanded. "He won't understand. He'll blame me." Her words turned into racking sobs.

"No, he won't. He'll be as sad as you are, but no one's to blame," Mrs. Griffen said, shaking her head as she gazed at the trees.

Ashleigh knew that wasn't true. She could have prevented the accident, but now it was too late. Midnight was going to die and there was nothing she could do to save him.

"Ashleigh," her mother finally said, turning back to face her daughter, "do you want to come and say goodbye to Midnight?"

The thought of seeing Midnight once more and then

never seeing him again terrified Ashleigh. "No," she said, shrinking back on the bed. "I can't do it."

"No one's going to make you." Mrs. Griffen looked concerned. "I just thought you'd want to."

"No." Ashleigh shook her head fiercely.

She stood up and walked over to the window, her back to her mother. A few of the broodmares were out grazing in the paddocks. It was a beautiful, sunny day. Dr. Frankel's Bronco was parked by the barn—the only sign that something was wrong.

"Is it going to happen right now?" Ashleigh asked, in barely a whisper.

"I don't think we should prolong this any more than we have to, do you?" her mother said quietly.

"Then will you say good-bye to him for me?" Ashleigh asked miserably, turning to flop facedown on her bed.

"Of course I will." Mrs. Griffen agreed. She hesitated, as if she was waiting for Ashleigh to change her mind. But Ashleigh lay still, her head buried in her quilt.

"Okay," Mrs. Griffen said finally. "I'd better go."

As soon as the door closed, Ashleigh turned over on her back and looked glassy-eyed at the ceiling. Feeling as though her heart might break into a thousand pieces, she heard her mother go downstairs. The screen door slammed shut, and then there was nothing but silence.

A little while later Dr. Frankel's Bronco started up

and drove away, and then Ashleigh heard the cough and splutter of the tractor as Jonas revved it up. It was over. Midnight was dead.

Ashleigh turned over, buried her face in the pillow, and wept. *I'll never see him again,* she thought miserably, *and I didn't even say good-bye.*

10

Though it was only afternoon, Ashleigh fell into a fitful sleep. Her dreams were filled with visions of Midnight—Midnight as a foal, Midnight in the paddocks, Midnight lying down with his cast. As Ashleigh tossed and turned in her sleep, the sound of hysterical whinnying filled her dreams. Midnight thrashed around in his stall, lashing out at every turn. He was in pain, he needed the shot. As Ashleigh got to the door of the barn, there was something barring her way, a sort of invisible wall. "I'm coming! I'm coming, Midnight!" she cried, but she couldn't get to him. Then suddenly the wall disappeared, and Ashleigh raced down the aisle. But Midnight wasn't there. All that was left was an empty stall.

Later that evening Ashleigh awoke to find that she had slept all afternoon and straight through dinner. Dragging herself out of bed, she got up to call Mona. She had to tell her what had happened.

"Ash?" Mona ventured when Ashleigh had finished her sad tale.

"Yeah?" Ashleigh sniffed. She didn't know when she'd ever stop crying.

"I know you may not want to hear this," Mona said. "But I think I know what will make you feel better."

"What?" Ashleigh gulped.

"Riding," Mona said. "We haven't gone in such a long time."

Ashleigh sighed. "I don't know, Mona." It *had* been a long time, and she'd been completely neglecting Stardust, but Ashleigh wasn't sure if she could face seeing Midnight's empty stall.

"What if I bring Frisky over tomorrow?" Mona suggested. "We can try it."

"All right," Ashleigh said, giving in. She hoped Mona was right. Maybe a good long trail ride was just what she needed.

When Mona led Frisky up Edgardale's drive the next afternoon, gray clouds hung ominously over the farm, and a rumble of thunder sounded in the distance. It looked like a storm was brewing. Ashleigh was waiting by the barn door with Stardust, all tacked up and ready to go. She hadn't even noticed the weather. Her parents had let her stay home from school, and she'd spent most of the day in her room, thinking about Midnight.

"Maybe we'd better wait until tomorrow," Mona said, looking at the sky. "It's going to pour any minute now."

But Ashleigh had been gearing herself up for this ride all day. Now that she'd decided to do it, it felt important—her first ride after Midnight's death, a chance to start over. She wasn't about to give it up because of a little rain.

"Just a quick ride, Mona," Ashleigh begged. "We can go back if it starts raining too hard."

Behind them, Stardust pawed the aisle impatiently.

Mona laughed. "Well, Stardust looks ready to get going," she said, and patted Frisky's neck. "We don't mind a little rain, do we, Frisky?"

Ashleigh undid the crossties and led Stardust out of the barn. The chestnut mare trotted past her, nearly yanking the reins out of Ashleigh's hands in her eagerness to get out.

"Whoa, girl," Ashleigh crooned. "Steady."

Mona was already up on Frisky's back.

"Want me to hold her for you while you mount up, Ash?" Mona offered.

"No, I'm all right," Ashleigh insisted. She took a firm hold on the reins, grabbed a handful of mane, and swung herself up into the saddle.

Just at that moment a strong gust of wind blew across the pastures and a flash of lightning streaked across the sky. Stardust started forward, catching Ashleigh by surprise. Before Ashleigh could stop her, Stardust tore the reins out of her hands and bolted across the grass like a bullet from a gun. The panic-stricken mare raced through an open gate and galloped across the paddock, heading for the white fence on the other side.

"Ashleigh!" Mona called after her.

"Easy," Ashleigh called to her mare. "Whoa, girl." But Stardust wasn't listening.

Keep calm, just keep calm, Ashleigh thought. She tried to turn, grabbing her left rein and applying pressure at the girth with her inside leg. But Stardust continued to gallop, and the panic rose in Ashleigh's throat as the white railing loomed dangerously close.

Please slow down, Ashleigh thought as her horse streaked across the grass. Then, just as they were about to crash into the fence, Stardust swerved left. There was nothing Ashleigh could do to stop herself from flying out of the saddle and landing hard on the ground.

Stardust didn't even pause to see if Ashleigh was all right before kicking up her heels and galloping off around the paddock. Ashleigh sat up, her heart pounding in her chest. She wasn't hurt, but the impact had stunned her a little.

"Ashleigh? Are you all right?" She heard voices calling, and through mud-splattered lashes she saw her family running across the grass toward her. In no time at all her parents were at her side. Caroline and Rory weren't far behind.

"Are you okay, Ashleigh?" Mrs. Griffen said, and knelt down beside her.

"I-I'm fine," Ashleigh stammered.

"Wow, Ash! What a big fall!" Rory exclaimed. He gazed admiringly at his sister, his eyes shining brightly.

"Don't start," she begged as her mother helped her to her feet. When Ashleigh saw the crushed look on Rory's face, she immediately felt guilty.

Ashleigh brushed off her jeans and looked across the paddock. Stardust was at a standstill now, sniffing the ground. She looked completely innocent. *Thanks a lot, Stardust,* Ashleigh thought. *Just what I needed.*

"She seems a little more settled now. She was probably just a little shaken up by the weather," Mrs. Griffen said kindly as Mona led the chestnut mare back over to Ashleigh. "Hop back on and walk her around."

"In a minute," Ashleigh answered. Her body was weak from crying over Midnight, and her legs felt like Jell-O. She knew it was best to get back on after a fall, but it was the last thing she felt like doing.

"Go on, Ashleigh," Mr. Griffen urged her.

"If you all would just leave me alone, I'd get back on, okay?" Ashleigh said under her breath, scowling.

"She gets nervous with everyone watching."

"All right, all right." Mr. Griffen raised his hands in the air. "We'll leave you to it."

Ashleigh watched as her family turned and walked across the grass, thoughts spinning around her mind. Her hands were trembling. *But I don't have to get back on Stardust now*, Ashleigh realized. *I can tell Mona I want to ride on my own, and take Stardust back to the barn instead. No one will know.*

It was starting to drizzle, and Ashleigh was cold. It didn't take her long to convince herself. As soon as Rory had disappeared into the house, Ashleigh turned to her friend and took a deep breath.

"Look, Mona, would you mind if I just took Stardust around the paddock on my own?" She tried to make her voice sound as normal as possible. "I know we said we'd ride together, but I think it might overexcite her if Frisky's around."

Mona looked surprised. "You don't think Stardust would be calmer if she had another horse for company?" she asked. "Do you want me to watch?"

"I think it'd be better if Stardust and I were alone for now, that's all," Ashleigh insisted. "We can go out together this weekend, maybe."

"Well, okay, if that's what you want." Mona shrugged. "I guess I'd better take Frisky home before it starts pouring. I'll see you at school, Ash."

"Thanks, Mona," Ashleigh said.

Ashleigh felt terrible as she watched her friend lead her horse off across the paddocks. Mona had really been looking forward to riding, and Ashleigh had been eager to get a fresh start after everything that had happened with Midnight. Stardust had managed to ruin everything.

Dusk was starting to creep across the farm, and Mona was just a shadowy figure by the time she and Frisky reached the edge of the property. Ashleigh waved, and then waited a few more minutes before unlatching the gate to the paddocks. She looked over her shoulder to make sure there was no one watching from the house. It looked like it was all clear.

"Okay, let's get you back to the barn, Stardust," Ashleigh said resolutely. She frowned as the mare nudged her shoulder. "Sorry," Ashleigh said, giving the reins a tug. "You can't make it up to me now. It's too late."

Ashleigh led Stardust back to her stall. Hastily she whisked off her tack and brushed the worst of the mud off the mare's coat. Stardust nipped Ashleigh playfully, but Ashleigh ignored her. Picking up her tack, she carried it out of the stall and down the aisle to the tack room.

Ashleigh rubbed a mud-smeared hand across her face. The rain was coming down in torrents now. She was going to have to make a run for it if she wanted to get to the house without getting soaked. She pulled her parka up over her head and set out across the drive.

When she reached the house, she ran up the steps and pushed open the screen door. Her father was hunched over some paperwork at the pine kitchen table, and Ashleigh stood still, waiting for him to say something. But he was too engrossed in what he was doing and didn't even look up. Ashleigh put some water on to boil and delved into the cupboard for the hot chocolate mix. Just as she banged the carton down onto the counter, Caroline came into the kitchen, brushing her long blond hair.

"So, how did it go out there with Stardust?" Caroline asked, raising her eyebrows.

"Yes, was she all right?" Mr. Griffen said, looking up.

"She was fine, just fine," Ashleigh said. She spooned some cocoa mix into her mug. "It was raining, so I only took her around for a few minutes, but she was okay."

As her father returned to his papers, Ashleigh grabbed her mug and made her way to her bedroom.

Caroline followed her, bouncing onto her bed and shaking a bottle of pink nail polish. Brow furrowed in concentration, she began to paint her toenails.

Ashleigh sat down on her own bed, careful not to disturb her kitten, who was asleep on her pillow. She balanced her mug on a pile of books on her bedside table.

"Hey, Ashleigh," Caroline said without looking up. "Can you clean up your side of the room at some point?"

"Oh, Caro," Ashleigh moaned. "Just because I don't have flowery perfume bottles and fashion magazines lying around—"

"Well, I'm sorry, but hoof oil doesn't belong in a bedroom," Caroline interrupted. "And your kitten—he sheds all over everything." She tossed a cushion at Ashleigh's bed, hitting Prince Charming. The kitten jumped up in a fright and fled the room.

"Oops," Caroline said, covering her mouth.

"He wasn't doing anyone any harm just sleeping there!" Ashleigh cried, her blood boiling. "He's only a baby. If you keep on scaring him, he won't want to come in here anymore."

"Ashleigh I know you're upset about Midnight," Caroline said, scooting around to look at Ashleigh. "And I'm sorry you fell off Stardust. I don't know why you didn't get back on, but don't take it out on me. After—"

"What did you say?" Ashleigh demanded.

"Nothing," Caroline said, looking guilty.

Ashleigh was ready to explode. Caroline must have seen her from the house. She opened her mouth to retaliate, and closed it again. No, she wouldn't let Caroline have the satisfaction of knowing she'd hit the nail on the head.

Ashleigh jumped to her feet, knocking against her

bedside table and spilling her hot chocolate. "Now look what you've made me do!" she cried.

She stormed out of the room and made her way downstairs to the phone in the den. Taking a deep breath, she dialed Mona's number, twisting the phone cord in her hands as she waited.

"Hi, Mrs. Gardener. Could I talk to Mona, please?"

Ashleigh waited for a few moments before Mona's concerned voice came over the line.

"Ashleigh, how are you doing? Was Stardust okay after I left?"

"Mona, I'm really sorry about earlier," Ashleigh apologized. But she couldn't bring herself to say the truth. "Stardust was fine. I rode her for ten minutes and then I took her back inside," she told her friend, repeating her fib.

"Well, that's good." Mona laughed. "I had a horrible feeling you weren't going to get back on again."

"What makes you say that?" Ashleigh asked guiltily.

"Oh, I don't know. Anyway, never mind—the main thing is that you did," Mona assured her. "Hey, sorry to bring this up, Ash, but you do remember that we're having another impossible math test tomorrow, right?"

"Oh, no," Ashleigh wailed. Math had been the last thing on her mind. What else could go wrong? "I guess I've got a few hours left to get some studying done," she sighed. "I'd better get moving."

Ashleigh put down the phone and took a deep breath. The math test was one more thing to worry about, but at the moment she felt worst about lying to everyone. She really should have gotten back on Stardust.

Through the window in the den, she could see the horse barn looming in the darkness. Ashleigh frowned. Midnight was gone forever, Stardust had dumped her on her first attempt at riding in a week, and her math grade was plummeting. *Why not give up horses altogether?* she thought. *Maybe I'd be better off.*

11

"Ashleigh, are you awake?" Caroline walked over and tried to peer into Ashleigh's face.

"Just leave me alone." Ashleigh pulled up her quilt and curled into a ball, wanting to go back to sleep. But a moment later she remembered everything that had happened. As it all came flooding back, Ashleigh felt a dull ache in her chest. She couldn't bear the thought of going out to the barn and seeing Stardust's pert little face and Midnight's empty stall. She rolled over in her bed, just lying there, quiet in her misery.

"Aren't you coming out to the barn this morning?" Caroline persisted.

"No," Ashleigh answered in a muffled voice.

"Well, what should I say to Mom and Dad?" Caroline asked.

"Say anything you want. I don't care." Ashleigh put her fingers in her mouth and bit down hard to stop the tears. Never before had she felt so completely alone.

Caroline didn't say anything more. Ashleigh watched out of the corner of her eye as her sister pulled a sweater on over her head and made for the door. When she heard Caroline run down the stairs, she turned her face into the pillow. There was no point in going down to the barn. Midnight was gone, and Ashleigh wouldn't mind if she never saw Stardust again. Besides, her family could manage without her.

As Ashleigh lay there she could hear her parents' voices in the kitchen and the bustling sounds of breakfast being prepared. *How can they all go on as though nothing happened?*

Ashleigh threw back the covers and got out of bed. She pulled on her jeans and sneakers and grabbed a sweater. Running down the stairs, she snatched up her backpack and was out the front door before anyone could stop her.

"Ashleigh!" Her mother's voice followed her, but Ashleigh wasn't stopping for anyone.

For the next few days Ashleigh stayed away from the barn. She got up in the morning, headed off for school, and came home again, watching TV or reading magazines to fill the hours before bedtime. At school, Ashleigh felt as though her friends were walking on eggshells around her. She understood that they didn't know how to comfort her, but it still hurt that they barely spoke to her at all.

On Thursday she stayed late at school, watching a basketball game to avoid going back to Edgardale. On the way home she sat on the bus beside Mona and stared silently out the window, feeling just as empty and dazed as she had the day Midnight died.

"Ashleigh," Mona said, and touched her elbow. Ashleigh nearly jumped out of her skin. She turned to look at her friend.

"I just wondered, could I come over and ride with you tomorrow?" Mona asked.

"No, I don't think so," Ashleigh said, trying to think of an excuse. "We're pretty busy with the yearlings and everything, you know."

"Oh." Mona looked hurt. "I know you have the sales to get ready for. It's just that I haven't been over to Edgardale for so long, that's all."

"Well, maybe some other time, okay?" Ashleigh rose to her feet. "I've got to go."

Ashleigh got off the bus and made her way up the drive to the farm. She gave the horse barn a wide berth, going directly into the house and up the stairs to her bedroom. She shut the door behind her, then got out her homework and spread it out on her desk.

At least I'll do better at school now that I'm not riding, Ashleigh thought. Her math test hadn't gone very well, but she was determined to do better on the next one. Yet when Ashleigh opened her notebook, she could only stare at the blank pages inside.

She picked up her pencil and, instead of copying out her first math homework problem, began to write a letter.

Dear Kira,

Sorry it's been so long. But a lot has been happening here. I went to see Lightning and she is doing great. But I . . .

Ashleigh lifted her pencil from the paper. She wasn't sure what to write next. There was no way to sound cheerful, but how could she send a sad letter to Kira, the bravest girl she knew? With her cancer, Kira had faced death every day. She didn't need to hear about Midnight.

Ashleigh ripped the page out of her notebook and crumpled it into a ball.

Over and over in her mind, she replayed images of Midnight's fight with Sparky: the two horses rearing up on their hind legs, Midnight twisting out of the way as Sparky tried to bite him. Ashleigh had cheered Midnight on, and now he was dead.

She was so far away with her thoughts that she didn't register the sound of the screen door slamming shut and feet padding up the stairs. She looked up as her mother came into the room.

"I just wanted to see if you were going to take Stardust out for a ride this afternoon," Mrs. Griffen said.

"No." Ashleigh shook her head and bent over to fumble around in her school bag. "I've got too much homework to do," she mumbled.

"Ashleigh," her mother said, and knelt down beside her. "How long is this going to go on?"

"What?" Ashleigh gave her a blank look.

"You know what I'm talking about," Mrs. Griffen insisted. "You haven't been in the barn for days now. We need your help out there."

"Caroline can do it for a change," Ashleigh said, turning away.

"Caroline has her own chores to do, and she has been helping—she's been taking care of Stardust for you," Mrs. Griffen said. "But, to be honest, she's not as good with the horses as you are. And there's Stardust to consider, too," she went on. "We agreed to keep her on the farm with the understanding that you would ride her and take care of her. Caroline's been grooming her and mucking out her stall, but Stardust needs exercise and attention. I can see you're feeling bad, but don't you want to ride?"

"No," Ashleigh said, staring at the wall.

"You can't give up after one fall, Ashleigh," Mrs. Griffen said encouragingly. "We all have bad days."

Suddenly Ashleigh felt herself collapsing under the weight of her own frustration. He mother had been

153

talking about Stardust, but Ashleigh's mind was still full of memories of Midnight.

"There's something I've got to tell you," she cried. "You know that first night, when you asked if any of us saw how Midnight's accident happened? Well, I did! I saw Midnight and Sparky attacking each other in the paddock. I should have stopped them. Caroline even said we should," she babbled on, "but I told her to leave them alone! I thought I knew best. Now Midnight's dead and it's all my fault. I'm so, so sorry!" she sobbed. "You see, I'm *not* good with the horses—I'm terrible! Midnight's gone because of me, and I can't even keep my own horse from dumping me!"

"Oh, Ashleigh," Mrs. Griffen said, taking Ashleigh in her arms. "Of course it wasn't your fault. Is this what you've been torturing yourself over?" She hugged Ashleigh tight. "None of us could have stopped those horses. They're playful, fragile creatures, in spite of their size. And accidents happen."

Ashleigh hung her head. Although she had finally confessed to seeing the accident, she felt none of the relief that should come after a confession. Midnight was still gone, forever.

"But he was special," Ashleigh insisted. "I can't just forget him."

"No one's asking you to forget him," Mrs. Griffen told her. "But you can't just give up, either. If you give

Stardust a chance, you might find that she's special, too.

"You had a bad start the other day," her mother went on. "The weather was terrible, and it wasn't Stardust's fault—it was just another accident." Mrs. Griffen stood up. "Come on, Ashleigh. It's dinnertime," she said.

Ashleigh nodded, wiping her face on her sleeve, and followed her mother downstairs. The table was set, and an uncomfortable silence filled the room as she sat down with her family.

"We had some good news today," Mr. Griffen announced. "The Fontaines were so pleased with Quest's run that they're talking about coming up to take a look at our yearlings. So maybe things will start picking up for us from now on," he said cheerfully.

"I hope so," Caroline said.

Ashleigh listened to them talk. She knew they were waiting for her to participate, but she just couldn't. She looked across the table at Rory. He was playing with his food, but he looked so sad, and he didn't even glance up from his plate. Ashleigh had been so wrapped up in her own grief she hadn't thought about her little brother, but he had loved Midnight, too. She wished she could make him feel better, but she wasn't sure how.

The following day Ashleigh again avoided the horses and the barn. She went through the motions of her day like a robot—going to school, coming home, doing her homework, eating her dinner, and then going to bed. On Saturday afternoon she was in her room, folding her sweatshirts and jeans into neat piles and putting them back in her closet, when Caroline burst into the room.

"Ashleigh, *what* are you doing?" Caroline asked, her eyes wide with surprise.

"Cleaning up," Ashleigh explained as she picked up the piles of clean clothes.

Caroline grabbed a shirt and began folding it neatly on Ashleigh's bed. "I don't know if you've noticed, but Prince Charming's been missing all day," she said, glancing at Ashleigh.

Ashleigh dropped the pair of socks she was rolling up. Prince Charming never left the house unless she took him somewhere. "What do you mean?" she asked. "I thought he was downstairs."

Caroline looked worried. "I know, but I haven't seen him anywhere," she explained.

Ashleigh bent down and looked under her bed. She found piles of books and old horse magazines, a pair of reins, and a bar of saddle soap, but no kitten. Then she checked under Caroline's bed. Nothing. Ashleigh ran out of the room and down into the den with Caroline close behind her. The two girls looked under the furniture and behind cushions. Then they checked the kitchen. Nothing.

"I think he may be out in the barn," Caroline suggested. "He likes it down there. Will you help me look?"

Ashleigh didn't stop to think. She ran out the screen door, across the drive, and into the barn, without even pausing at Midnight's old stall.

"Prince Charming?" she called, searching up and down the aisle. Caroline followed her as they peered into the broodmares' empty stalls. All the horses were still out in the paddocks, and the kitten was nowhere in sight.

Ashleigh headed for the tack room. When she opened the door, there was a flash of gray and white striped fur as the little kitten jumped out. Ashleigh picked him up and hugged him close, spinning around to meet her sister's guilty gaze.

"He was right here!" she said, stroking the kitten's soft fur.

"I-I know," Caroline stammered, looking ashamed. "I put him there."

Ashleigh glared at her sister. "You did?" she asked, but Caroline was acting so strange that Ashleigh felt more curious than angry.

"Ash, I need your help," Caroline explained. "I didn't know how else I could get you down here. You've been so stubborn about not going into the barn."

Ashleigh held her purring kitten tight and shrugged. "What for?" she asked.

"It's Stardust," Caroline said. The two girls looked at each other intently for a moment. Then Ashleigh put Prince Charming back in the tack room, closing the door behind him. She'd take him back to the house later. Now she wanted to hear what was going on.

"All right," she said, turning to Caroline with a resigned sigh. "What's wrong?"

"Come on, I'll show you," Caroline said.

The two girls leaned on the gate to the paddock Stardust shared with Moe. The pretty chestnut mare was standing by the opposite fence, her head weaving slightly from side to side, her neck stretched out low as she stared into space. Behind her, Moe was feasting on the longer grass near the fence posts. Then Stardust began gnawing on the fence, her teeth working the painted wood until it began to splinter. At that moment Ashleigh realized Stardust was bored—bored and depressed.

"Look at her," Caroline said. "I don't know what to do, Ash. She hasn't been eating her grain, and she just stands there weaving and cribbing like that—she does it in her stall, too."

Ashleigh tried not to hear the desperation in Caroline's voice. She didn't want to see Stardust or care about how pathetic the mare looked. But she couldn't help it. She unlatched the gate and went into the paddock.

"Hey, Stardust," she called, walking over to the mare and holding out her hand.

Stardust lifted her head and looked at Ashleigh. Pricking her ears, she nickered.

"Good girl," Ashleigh crooned as she walked across the grass.

Stardust took one step in Ashleigh's direction, and then another and another. Soon they were face-to-face, and Ashleigh reached up to stroke her mare's forehead.

"It's all right, I'm here now," she soothed. She took hold of Stardust's halter and led her toward the barn. "Caro, will you get some carrots from the house? I want to see if I can get her to eat," Ashleigh explained to her sister, who was waiting at the gate.

Caroline smiled. "Of course," she said, spinning around and taking off at a run. "I'll be right back!"

Back in her stall, Ashleigh stood by Stardust's head as the mare sniffed her bucket of sweet feed. Caroline rested her elbows on the stall door and peered in at them anxiously.

Ashleigh broke off a bit of carrot and held it out. Stardust examined it with her lips, rolling it around on Ashleigh's palm before crunching it between her teeth.

"There," Ashleigh said, scooping up some of the sweet feed in her hand and placing another bit of carrot on top. "Now try this."

Stardust inspected Ashleigh's hand and lipped the carrot delicately.

"Come on," Ashleigh encouraged. "All of it—grain too."

Again Stardust took the bit of carrot between her teeth and chewed it noisily. Ashleigh was about to give up and drop the handful of sweet feed on the stall floor when Stardust's big pink tongue flicked out and the mare began slurping up the grain in Ashleigh's palm.

Ashleigh took three more carrots out of her pocket and broke them up into Stardust's feed bucket, on top of the grain. The mare watched her expectantly, as if she was waiting for Ashleigh to do something.

Ashleigh laughed and picked up the bucket. "Only for you, girl, and just this once." She raised the bucket to Stardust's nose, and the mare dove in with gusto, spraying sweet feed all over Ashleigh as she chewed.

"I knew you could do it!" Caroline exclaimed, beaming at her sister.

Ashleigh grinned and looked up at Stardust, whose nose was sticky with grain. "If you promise me you'll eat your breakfast, I'll take you out for a ride tomorrow," she said to the mare.

Stardust nudged Ashleigh's shoulder and then went back to her grain. Ashleigh waited as the mare licked the bucket clean, happily breathing in the sweet horse smells that she had missed so much.

12

Ashleigh's alarm went off early the next morning. She pressed the button down with a *thwack* and lay very still under her comforter. It was dark and cold, but she couldn't wait to get up. She counted to three and then flung back the covers and leaped out of bed, shivering as she felt the cold wood floor under her bare feet. Caroline hadn't stirred. Ashleigh scrambled into her clothes and slipped out of the room. The house was quiet as she hurried down the stairs and pushed open the screen door. As she made her way to the barn she could hear the horses shuffling in their stalls and nickering for their breakfasts. She went right to Stardust's stall and looked in over the door.

"Hey, you," Ashleigh called to the sleeping mare. Stardust's eyes fluttered open and she struggled to her feet when she heard Ashleigh's voice. "Breakfast time," Ashleigh said, pulling bits of straw from Stardust's forelock as the mare nudged her hands for treats.

Ashleigh's parents didn't seem to know what to say when they found her mucking out Stardust's stall. Ashleigh quickly broke the silence.

"I thought I might take Stardust out for a quick ride when I'm done. Is that all right?"

"A ride?" Mr. Griffen said, stopping his wheelbarrow in the aisle.

"Uh-huh. Is there something wrong?" Ashleigh asked.

"No, not at all," her mother explained, her green eyes wide with surprise. "It's just that we weren't expecting it. I mean, you haven't even been out here in the barn in days, let alone ridden."

"It's about time," Jonas said in a mock gruff voice, grinning at Ashleigh as he came up the aisle behind them.

"Ash, are you going for a ride? Can I come?" Rory piped up as he emerged from Moe's stall.

"Not today, Rory," Mrs. Griffen said. "I'll help you mount up once you're ready, Ashleigh."

"Rory can come if he wants," Ashleigh offered.

"Yes!" Rory said, punching the air.

Ashleigh laughed and walked down the aisle to where Stardust was waiting in crossties. "Hey, girl," Ashleigh murmured as she rubbed the mare's nose. "I bet you're dying to go out, aren't you?" Stardust snorted, as if in response, and Ashleigh laughed. "All right, let's get going."

When Rory was ready, they brought their horses outside to mount up. Ashleigh started to feel her nerves returning. She concentrated on what Sally had said about trusting Stardust, and tried to get a grip on herself. This time when Stardust tried to move away, Ashleigh stood firm.

She was already swinging herself up into the saddle when her mother came out to help. Mrs. Griffen gave Rory a leg up and then turned to look up at Ashleigh.

"Don't just stand there staring, Mom," Ashleigh said, smiling. "You're making me nervous."

"All right. Well, I'll see you later." Mrs. Griffen laughed and walked off toward the house. Then she called back over her shoulder, "Have fun, you two."

As they walked down the grassy paddock lanes, Ashleigh felt a tingle of nervous excitement. Stardust was raring to go and was tugging at the bit, but Ashleigh kept a firm hold on the reins as the mare tried to break into a trot. Stardust settled back down again and walked forward.

A bird flew up out of the hedgerow, and Ashleigh felt the mare tense up again. She leaned down and patted Stardust's coppery neck. "You're all right, girl," she called, and loosened her grip on the reins. Stardust snorted and stretched out her neck, walking forward confidently. *Maybe Sally was right,* Ashleigh thought. *Stardust will be good if I trust her first.*

Ashleigh nudged Stardust forward into a trot toward the open stretches of pasture. Rory came up alongside her, grinning as he posted to Moe's quick trot.

"Do you feel like going a little faster?" Ashleigh asked him.

"Definitely," Rory cried.

Ashleigh hesitated. "Well, I'll lead off at a canter. Tell me if it's too fast, though, okay?"

"Don't worry, Ashleigh." Rory grinned. "We like to go fast, too."

Ashleigh nudged Stardust on with her heels and felt the power of the horse surging beneath her as they cantered across the grass. As she rocked to Stardust's easy canter, Ashleigh could hardly believe she'd almost given up riding. She had forgotten how much she loved it.

As they headed out onto the open stretches of pasture, Ashleigh pushed Stardust faster, into a hand gallop. She leaned low and fed the reins up the mare's neck. The wind whipped her face, and she felt a thrill of exhilaration flood through her. It was as if the wind was blowing the pain and trouble of the past few months out of her system. There was nothing like it.

Ashleigh was so caught up in the thrill of the gallop that she'd hardly been paying attention to how far they'd ridden. But she knew she couldn't leave Rory too far behind. She pulled Stardust up to a trot and then a walk, and soon heard Rory cantering up behind them.

Ashleigh patted Stardust's neck. "Good girl," she crooned. Stardust snorted, her ears pricked forward. She seemed to be enjoying herself as much as Ashleigh.

"Wow, Ash," Rory said breathlessly, easing Moe down to a walk beside her. "That was fun!"

In the cold air, their horses' breaths floated up in little white clouds. Ashleigh sat back in the saddle and breathed deeply, feeling better than she had in a long time.

"That *was* fun, Rory," she said, turning to her brother. "But we have to get back. I need to call Mona, and maybe we can help Jonas work with the yearlings today, too."

"Good idea," Rory cried. "Let's go!"

Ashleigh reached forward to hug Stardust's neck. "And guess what, girl?" she murmured to her horse. "I'm going to use the money I won on Quest's race to get a special nameplate for your stall, with both our names engraved on it!"

As soon as she had finished putting Stardust away, Ashleigh rushed to the phone to call Mona.

"You know, Mona, I was thinking," Ashleigh said when her friend picked up. "Do you want to come over to ride tomorrow after school? I mean, I know I said my parents were busy with the yearlings, but—"

"I'd love to," Mona interrupted, sounding relieved.

"There's something else I wanted to say," Ashleigh said hesitantly. "You know when we were in Florida, before Midnight died? When I saw how much Quest loved running that race, I knew how much Midnight would have hated not being able to gallop or race. I just couldn't admit it until now," she explained.

"I hadn't thought about it like that," Mona said, "but you're right."

"I just wanted you to know that I haven't forgotten him," Ashleigh said. "But there's another horse who needs me now—someone I've been kind of neglecting."

"That wouldn't be Stardust by any chance, would it?" Mona teased, and Ashleigh laughed.

"Anyway, I'll tell you more about it tomorrow. I have to go—Rory's waiting for me," Ashleigh explained. "There's something we have to do. I'll see you at school tomorrow."

Ashleigh and Rory walked down the lanes between the paddocks and out into the pastures behind. Between them they struggled with the little fir tree they'd bought that afternoon at the nursery in Lexington. It was four o'clock and the light was starting to fade as they made their way across the grass.

"It's not far now, Rory," Ashleigh said.

"Good, 'cause I'm tired," Rory answered.

Ashleigh smiled. She felt a little sad, but she was glad for Rory's company. They were going to do something she'd been meaning to do for some time now—visit the spot on the farm where Midnight had been buried. For days Ashleigh had chastised herself for not saying good-bye to Midnight, and this was her way of making amends.

They walked across the pastures and up a hill to a beautiful meadow overlooking Edgardale, where they came upon the mound of freshly turned-up earth.

"Well, here it is, Rory," Ashleigh said quietly. She felt tears well up in her eyes, and she blinked them away. "Let's get to work." She put the sapling down on the ground and pulled out two small spades from her jeans pockets.

When the hole was about a foot deep they both stopped digging and lowered the little tree into the ground. With gentle hands they pushed the earth back around the roots and patted it down. Then they stood up to look at their handiwork.

The little tree stood out in the middle of the meadow. It was small now, but Ashleigh hoped it would grow strong and tall. It would probably be at Edgardale a lot longer than they would.

"We'll never forget you, Midnight," Ashleigh murmured.

She looked over at Rory and saw the tears rolling down his cheeks. "Don't be sad," she said, wrapping her arm around him. "Midnight wouldn't want that."

"Do you think he can see us, Ash?" Rory asked in a quiet, serious voice.

"Maybe," Ashleigh said. "Anyway, I'm sure he likes his tree—not that the tree would stand a chance if Midnight could get to it. He'd probably eat it all up."

"You're right," Rory said quietly. "He was pretty silly like that, wasn't he?"

Ashleigh smiled. It was good to be able to talk about Midnight. For so long she'd winced at the mention of his name.

"Come on, Rory," Ashleigh said, taking her brother's hand. "You can help me put that nameplate on Stardust's stall."

OLIVIA COATES grew up in England surrounded by horses. As a child, she rode in equitation and jumping classes. Now she makes her living as an author, writing about the animals she loves best. She lives in London with a dog and two cats, but always finds the time to ride horses in the countryside. An avid racing fan, she has written seven novels for young adults.